Having spent his childhood in Cheltenham, David Wiltshire went on to complete his National Service in Aden and Singapore. He then returned to England to work as a dentist and now lives with his wife in Bedford.

SCENT OF MADNESS

As Lieutenant Tom O'Hara investigates several gruesome murders in a large teaching hospital, a wave of terror about the escalating severity of the situation is sweeping through the nursing staff. Despite the obscene dissection of the victims' bodies, there are forensic clues pointing to the killer. O'Hara suspects a soldier who was brought back from Afghanistan in a coma. The man is the victim of a torture he associates with the scent of roses worn by a sinister and unseen woman. The scent, unfortunately, is identical to that worn by Dr Jean Hacker, who works at the same hospital . . .

DAVID WILTSHIRE

SCENT OF MADNESS

Complete and Unabridged

ULVERSCROFT
Leicester

First published in Great Britain in 2012 by
Robert Hale Limited
London

First Large Print Edition
published 2013
by arrangement with
Robert Hale Limited
London

The moral right of the author has been asserted

British Library CIP Data

Wiltshire, David, 1935 –
Scent of madness.
1. Suspense fiction.
2. Large type books.
I. Title
823.9'14–dc23

ISBN 978-1-4448-1465-1

Published by
F. A. Thorpe (Publishing)
Anstey, Leicestershire

Set by Words & Graphics Ltd.
Anstey, Leicestershire
Printed and bound in Great Britain by
T. J. International Ltd., Padstow, Cornwall

For Paul and Chris Forster.
Thanks for the memories.

Prologue

Slowly, it just appeared. It was like something in a child's magic-painting book, emerging from the surrounding blackness.

Except this was no child's painting, but a terrible head from the nightmare regions of the human mind.

Two eyes glittered behind the 'V' shaped slits in a woollen hood.

Eyes that burned with a fierce madness.

Eyes that she instantly recognized.

She was paralysed with fear, not just from terror, but the unfairness of life, and the even greater unfairness of death — the terrible death that she knew this thing would inflict upon her.

1

He returned to earth at night descending at seven hundred feet per minute on a three degree glide slope, unaware in his coma-like state of the myriad sprawling lights of the city passing below.

As the Military Transport turned onto its final approach the pilot called to traffic control —

'Tower, Spectre four-seven. Finals with the gear.' The radio crackled —

'Roger Spectre four-seven. Clear land runway two-eight. Wind two seven zero at eight knots. 'Follow me' awaits at first 'high speed'.'

He spoke over his shoulder to the load-master standing behind him next to the flight engineer.

'Right, get them settled down the back — especially the casovac people.'

The loadie descended the short metal steps to the cavernous hold, its dimly lit interior filled with the roar of the four jet engines.

Rows of troops were sitting together, some in the sand coloured camouflage fatigues of the desert, others in rough civilian dress, old suit jackets over dirty jeans, worn for the months they had been up-country in Afghanistan.

These were the men of the Special Forces coming home from the war on terror, back for an in-depth debrief, and keen to check for themselves that some bureaucratic foul-up had not listed them killed in action. Then, maybe a few Buds . . .

All except one had his mind set on getting back to the good old US of A.

He was in his own world.

A world of madness, of terrors unknown to his conscious being.

The loadmaster moved down the rows of men until he reached the medical team, glancing at the inert figure with the saline drip entering his arm. He shouted above the roar of the engines.

'We'll be touching down soon. Strap yourselves in.'

He moved on, then, satisfied everything was secure, he informed the flight deck via the intercom.

The pilot, in khaki-coloured flying suit with squadron patches, gently held one gloved hand on the throttles as he watched the boundary lights flash beneath him. Over the runway he pulled back on the stick and flared out the aircraft, setting it down with a gentle

4

shudder on the mile-long well lit strip of concrete.

After the last few months of night landings on desert strips it was a piece of cake.

The smooth flight was interrupted by the thumping vibrations of contact with the runway as the over one hundred ton weight of the plane settled.

The aircraft easily made the first high speed turnoff.

From the shadows at the side of the well-lit runway a van appeared bearing an illuminated sign reading, 'Follow Me'.

The Transport turned off the main apron some three-quarters of a mile from the terminal and taxied to a collection of buildings.

The pilot responded to the ground-crew's baton, and braked to a halt. He set the parking brake, and signalled to the loadie to open the rear ramp and doors.

Hydraulics whined and in less than a minute the gurney with the patient attached to the drip and a monitor was brought down the ramp and wheeled towards a waiting ambulance.

An officer followed, he took the unconscious man's hand in both of his and looked down at the face, seeing again the vicious wound across one cheek that was now crudely stitched, and knowing the other injuries the man had sustained said softly 'God be with you, James.'

He straightened up, saluted the prone figure, then faced the civilian paramedics. His voice now had a decisive edge. 'Take good care of him.' With that he returned into the depths of the aircraft.

The reception crew took the brief medical notes and completed the handover.

'Why has he come to us and not to a military hospital?' asked a paramedic as he signed the formal acceptance sheet.

The airforce attendant shrugged.

'We've got another two hours flight — rough weather over the mountains. Seems your place agreed to take him. He needs to be in critical care as soon as possible.'

With the blue emergency sign flashing, but no siren, the vehicle moved off, heading towards the City's University Hospital.

Before the little convoy had reached the exit gate the plane was taxiing again, the ramp still closing whilst it was on the move.

With the loadmaster's crackled message that all was secure, the pilot requested the tower for immediate departure.

Permission was given and he acknowledged it with his call sign.

'Spectre four-seven — clear to go.'

Less than fifteen minutes after it had landed the Transport lifted off, its strobe light flashing amongst the stars until, receding, it was indistinguishable in the twinkling backdrop of the firmament.

And as it worked its way towards the hospital the repeating blue light of the ambulance was finally lost in the twinkling lights of the city.

The vehicle backed up to the ER entrance and, with a professional routine born of daily practice, they transferred the patient out of the back, pushing the trolley through the automatic doors and then quickly on down the corridor. They were met by a staff nurse, who walked alongside, frowning as she ran a practiced eye over the patient.

Puzzled, she looked down at the dreadfully scarred face with the inept suturing.

'What have we got here then?'

The senior paramedic gave her the documents. 'It's some sort of army casualty — in a coma. We were directed to the airport to meet a casovac. Control said you knew about it?'

The frown increased as she bent forward, taking a closer look at the face. 'Vital signs?'

The paramedic rattled them off.

'B.P. one thirty over eighty, breathing regular, deep, no external haemorrhages.'

The nurse shook her head — 'B.P. is too high for a normal coma.'

The paramedic nodded his agreement.

'I gather he has been in the hands of the Taliban — God knows what they did to him.'

Two more nurses joined the briskly moving group. The staff nurse pointed at a wide open door.

'In there, please.'

They entered an area that was equipped like a miniature operating room. With a combined effort the inert figure was transferred, fully supported and with the drip intact, onto the table.

'You two — remove his clothes. Cut them off. We don't know what we've got here.'

The young student nurses set about their task as Staff unpinned an army treatment card attached to the cotton shirt that had been revealed when the blanket was removed.

She gave it to the intern who had now arrived. He checked it against their notes while the paramedics waited.

The doctor turned the document over and found a name. 'Get a hospital tag on him. Apparently he's one James Larsson.' Working carefully, they cut his shirt free and began to remove it.

'Now then James — or is it Jim. What have you been up to?'

But the general air of work-a-day good humour was dispelled as the Resident in ER entered the room and stared down at the patient with the rest of them.

The man's body was lean, almost under-nourished; the muscles well developed but not excessively so, more the ropey thongs of a well-trained athlete.

But it was not that which held their attention. It was what had been done to him.

The Staff nurse spoke first. 'He's been tortured.'

The Resident ordered a Catscan, and confirmed he was not presenting as a true coma. It then took several hours, with many medical disciplines involved before James Larsson, still in his unknown hell, was wheeled into Critical Care and plumbed into the paraphernalia that is modern survival medicine.

The nurses on duty regularly checked their charge and the equipment, listening with satisfaction to the electric ping of the cardiac monitor as it steadily rode through the long night hours.

Every now and again one of them would delicately raise one of his closed eyelids, and check the reaction of his pupil to a beam of light.

It twitched, but remained wide: a black

shaft straight down into a skull to a brain that seemed devoid of life.

★ ★ ★

The large detached house, set in an acre of grounds was at the top of a private, gravelled road at the very edge of the city. Nearly all its rear windows looked out onto a forest that went on for nearly twenty miles.

In the upstairs master-bedroom a woman in her early thirties sat putting the finishing touches to her appearance.

She was of striking appearance, beautiful, and yet in no way stereotyped.

Her nose was well defined and she had a generous firm mouth. Her eyes were alive with the green fire of her Conomara grandmother's portrait in the living-room, but her angular cheeks spoke of the blood of her New England father.

Above the finely arched eyebrows, her chestnut hair often fell in a chaotic tumble to her shoulders, but was now — as for every workday — firmly drawn into a chignon.

She needed little make-up, the warm hue of her skin complimenting the redness of her hair. She used some eye-shadow to accentuate the colour of her pupils, and red to lips that were acclaimed, behind her back, by male colleagues and students alike.

Just for a faltering second, Dr Jean Hacker paused, wondered, as she did everyday now, why her husband couldn't love her — if only in the biblical sense? Was she so unattractive to him? Why the hell had he married her in the first place?

Picking up a cardigan, Jean Hacker grabbed her bag and left the room, pulling the door firmly shut behind her.

Downstairs in the kitchen she found her husband was already up, sipping coffee and reading the paper propped before him on the breakfast bar.

He did not look up as she entered. Determinedly cheerful she said, 'Good morning, Steven.'

He mumbled something as she made for the kettle and placed it on the hob. It re-boiled quickly as she put a slice of bread in the toaster.

'Have you had something to eat?'

He looked up, rearranging the paper as he said,

'Yes — thank you. Waffles.'

It was all so mechanical, so devoid of affection.

In the beginning, in the first few months, he had been so kind, attentive and loving. Then it was as if he had just lost interest. But

11

looking back, she realized it had begun after he'd been away for a convention.

She'd wondered if he'd had an affair. When she'd challenged him, he'd denied it, and things had improved for a while. Now, his behaviour was odd, rather than suspicious. There had never been a trace of another woman on his clothing.

Then a few weeks ago, he'd come home late one night and they had had a terrible row. He'd ended up sleeping in a guest bedroom.

Jean had spent the night crying her heart out, but had at last come to the conclusion there must be someone else.

In complete silence she buttered her toast, made her tea and sat down at the pine table.

Less than a minute later, Steven Hacker folded the paper, stood up, left the kitchen and went upstairs.

She'd finished when he came down and began to open the front door. She lowered her cup to the saucer, calling out —

'Steven.'

He paused, back to her.

'Yes.'

Her eyes suddenly welled up with moisture —

'I want a divorce.'

Slowly he turned around, found her gaze with his. Weirdly, for a second, some emotion passed over his face — love, anger, hatred — it was too fleeting for her to be sure what it was. But any emotion was a rarity. For a second she hoped, then,

'If that's what you want, I shan't stand in your way.'

Disappointed she said defiantly —

'We shall have to sell the house.'

He nodded — 'So be it.'

'That's that, then.' She was on the verge of bursting into tears when he said something that left her with no hope — for the future, or the past. It came out of the blue.

'Just one thing, who is it you are having an affair with? It's somebody at the hospital, isn't it?'

Stunned, she shook her head. 'There is no one else, Steven, never has been.'

Nodding, he smiled, knowingly.

'You make all the arrangements. I'll just sign.' The door clicked behind him.

Jean felt the tears welling up in her eyes, but there was no time to wallow in her misery. She worked at the same hospital as her husband as a lowly clinical assistant in the ER and also as an anesthesiologist on a sessional basis, the sort of appointments she had managed to secure when Steven had been given his residency in the Department of Oral Medicine.

The University Hospital was a vast collection of buildings, in fact a small town in which well over two and half thousand people worked: teaching, healing, nursing in its many departments; where patients occupied the nine hundred beds, while others cooked, cleaned, typed, lived, loved, and even died around them.

The Medical School and the Department of Anatomy were redbrick Victorian buildings with ornate stone embellishments and Latin inscriptions.

They were connected by a tunnel, the wall of which was lined with green and white glazed tiles. Half-way along its length another turned off and made for the main hospital. It became wide, better lit, and displayed mosaics depicting scenes of medical history. At its end, other tunnels wandered off like the spokes of a wheel — conveying the hurrying throng of medical students, in short white coats, and nurses and technicians from the two tower blocks above to the operating rooms, laboratories, other departments and kitchens.

Above one tunnel, the morning rush-hour was in full swing, the road gridlocked with traffic, the sidewalks full of hurrying preoccupied pedestrians, unaware of the shroud-covered corpses being wheeled on gurneys beneath their feet to the autopsy rooms.

In one, fourth-year clinical students were gathered in the small viewing galleries. They had a clear view of the stainless steel benches equipped with drainage gullies and grilles set in the floor below.

The room smelt of disinfectant and formaldehyde but this scarcely covered the odour of blood and faeces.

At 8.30 a.m. the first of six cases that would take place before mid-day had already commenced, the pathologist intoning mechanically into the microphone hanging from the ceiling: he had opened the forty-six year old woman's abdomen and chest with the classic 'Y'shaped incision holding the scalpel in heavy rubber gloved hands.

Dr Charles Seigle was a big, thickset man, dressed in surgical green scrubs, plus gown, and hat but no mask; his feet were encased in white rubber boots.

But any operating-room atmosphere was destroyed by the dark-brown shiny apron he wore, the lack of anesthesiologist or nurse, and the steady flow of red-clouded water from the gaping wound as the assistant gently played a hosepipe over the white flesh.

There was a constant gurgling from the drain beneath the doctor's feet. He had already lifted the heart and lungs from the wide-open chest cavity. Now, deftly, Seigle lifted out the woman's liver, played around with it in one hand, seeming to be judging its weight as he selected a fine cleaver, and then proceeded to cut it down the middle. He set aside the instrument, opened the bisected organ and offered it for display to the gallery and the closed-circuit television camera.

'Cirrhosis — classical. The female liver is very much more vulnerable.'

His dark eyes swept the rows of students, finally alighting on two females in the first row. Seigle's voice was heavy with sarcasm — 'Ah, career women. You are the ones, or rather your sisters in big business, who are at the greatest risk in modern times.'

He looked around again at his audience.

'How many units a week can the ladies safely imbibe?'

A tired chorus told him, 'Fourteen'.

He nodded.

'The desire for equality and the stress of proving you've got bigger balls than the men in your chosen career are responsible for several million women in this country drinking far more than that.'

His dark eyes settled again on the two girls with their open notebooks on their laps.

'There is a temptation to match men drink for drink, a dangerous pursuit for women whose physical tolerance to alcohol is far lower.'

The girls exchanged knowing looks. Dr Charles Seigle, Senior Pathologist was well known for his womanizing; this, combined with a rather arrogant, thinly disguised contempt for the opposite sex, was one of the reasons why — they guessed — he was still a bachelor at 42. Seigle was a domineering, vaguely menacing creature to some of the younger students.

'Here we go again,' groaned one.

She wasn't to be disappointed. Seigle's voice took on its characteristic edge.

'Women are not just men with hooters as you people should well know by now. They are a totally different animal — it's the biochemistry.'

There was the usual mocking sound from the males present. One of the girls whispered to the other, 'I heard one of the nurses talking about him. Seems she went out to a barbecue with him and he came on really strong. She walked home rather than go back in his car.'

Seigle set aside the liver and returned to the gaping abdomen — 'The pancreas of course is involved . . . '

It was another half an hour before he finished, leaving his assistant to suture up the 'Y' shaped incision. He peeled off his gloves and threw them into a pedal waste-bin, following them with his hat before untying and lifting the apron over his head.

He was scrubbing his hands when a head came round the door.

'Ah Charles, how are you placed for a game of squash later?'

The speaker's head lacked hair at the top which was shiny skin. The eyes behind the rimless glasses were big, and slate blue. Somewhere in his forties, Simon Limbach was not as broad as Seigle, but was taller, nearly 6 foot 4 inches and obviously fit: a cardio-thoracic surgeon, he was also a lay preacher.

The pathologist continued lathering his thick hairy forearms.

'Well now, what time are you thinking about?'

The light flashed on Limbach's glasses.

'4.30 OK?'

Seigle ran his arms one at a time under the jet of water to remove the soap.

'I've got to be out at 6.'

He gave a sly smile.

'Dining with the new psychiatrist, then I'm taking her to the opera.'

Limbach frowned.

'That didn't take you long. What's her name again?'

'Pam Mortimer.'

Charles Seigle elbowed off the water jet and reached for a paper towel.

'O.K., see you on the court.'

Limbach nodded.

'Fine.'

With that he was gone. Seigle worked the pedal bin with his foot and flung the balled paper inside, then pushed through into the locker-room and pulled his smock over his head.

His massive chest was covered in black hair. Seigle caught a glimpse of himself in the mirror on the inside of his locker door.

He grunted, released his green pants and let them fall to the floor. When he'd first met Pam Mortimer, he had had a feeling about her, like he had about Jean Hacker. Only the latter was untouchable, thanks to her prissy attitude to marriage. Everybody knew that things weren't right there: that fiery one was too much for that wimp of a husband. What she needed was a real man.

Simon Limbach's lanky frame and sloping stride ate up the four hundred yards of tunnel to the row of elevators at the bottom of tower block north. He joined the crowd as they surged forward as, with a 'ping' the doors of the nearest elevator opened.

He stood in the back corner, riding all the

way to the fourteenth floor, enjoying the ebb and flow of staff and students at each stop.

He was now in charge of the surgical budget and it was with this in mind that, high above the hurly-burly of the floors below and now the sole occupant of the elevator, that he finally stepped onto the carpeted open-plan offices where the Administration and Medical Secretaries were housed.

He passed three desks before stopping at one where a woman was typing a letter on a computer.

'Marjorie. Good morning.'

Startled, the woman looked up.

'Sorry, I didn't see you coming. Good morning, Simon.'

Limbach beamed. 'Deep into my correspondence so early?'

Marjorie Gooding was his secretary, at 38 still a spinster, and much in love with her boss, she revelled in the reflected glory of being his secretary. She pulled back into place one of the escaped strands of her blonde hair held with a dark leather comb at the nape of her neck.

Her long thin hands and delicate features were attractive to Simon Limbach, who, however, had never revealed this to anyone — denying it even to his puritan self.

She looked up at him. 'I'm afraid I didn't

stay after 7 last night. I don't like being here after dark when nearly everybody's gone. This floor gets very deserted and what with all the troubles . . . '

Limbach's thick eyebrows furrowed. They were having a lot of problems at the moment.

Apart from the increase of violence against the staff in the course of their duty, especially in ER, there had been two well-publicized attacks on nurses. Not surprising, when you had over one thousand nubile young women to look after that included technicians, physiotherapists, female students and ancillary workers as well as the nursing staff. It was a veritable honey pot for the male population of the city.

He placed a reassuring hand on her shoulder, well aware that the two brutal attacks had upset everybody.

'Don't ever stay late on my account, Marjorie. I'll never forgive myself if anything happened to you.'

She felt she could hardly breathe. For the first time he'd actually revealed how he felt, deep down, about her. The fact that he was already married never got in the way of her obsession with him.

He went on, 'I have a meeting with the board in an hour. I shall raise the whole question of security again and see if we can

21

squeeze some more money from the budget. I shall point out that incidents of this kind cause bad publicity in the media. People will choose to go elsewhere if we're not careful.'

She was hardly listening, as he rambled on about the terrible times they were living in. Marjorie Gooding finally managed to say breathlessly, 'Thank you, Simon.'

He straightened up.

'I'm just popping in to warn the Dean's secretary that I will be a few minutes late. I'm taking the Professorial round for the new bunch of clinical students, just a quick intro. He's gone to a seminar in Edinburgh in Scotland. I'll go through the letters with you at about 12 if that's all right?'

'Of course.'

He hurried away, throwing a 'Bye' over his shoulder.

She gazed adoringly at his retreating back before returning once more to the task of making herself indispensable in the life of Simon Limbach, M.D.

It was pure coincidence that the letter she was typing concerned a patient he'd seen a few days previously, who was now in the elevator of the other tower block ascending towards the floors housing the nurses' rooms.

George Nieminen was employed as an engineer at the hospital, based in the underground generating room from where pipes of many sizes spread out like arteries to all parts of the hospital and Medical School, taking energy to every building, every floor, every corridor, every *room*, the very cells of the man-made organism.

The letter was to Nieminen's insurance company, confirming that he'd been seen on the fourteenth and that the pain in his chest was referred, probably due to gallstones.

Nieminen was dressed in white coveralls with his hospital security badge and photograph clipped to his lapel. At his feet was the foldout workbox he carried to jobs all over the hospital.

His hair was greasy and unkempt falling darkly about an angular face that was pockmarked on the high cheekbones. When his lips parted, they revealed ill kept, chipped teeth.

As more nurses crowded in at one floor his piercing eyes swept over them. He could smell their sweet bodies, the heady mixture of perfume mixed with antiseptics and their warm young flesh.

Such was his daydreaming that he nearly missed his floor. The hardness in his groin he was able to cover as he lifted his workbox and stumbled out of the elevator.

Opposite was a security desk manned by an elderly woman.

'Come about a leaking radiator,' he said.

She checked a clipboard in front of her and then stood up.

'Room nineteen. Follow me.'

As he trailed behind, he shot quick glances into any half-open doors. In one he saw a girl in her slip.

The woman stopped and knocked on a door, holding her head close to the wood, listening. She knocked again then half-turned back to him.

'Hang on a second.'

She opened the door with a passkey.

'Hello — anyone in?' She asked.

There was no reply. She pushed it wide and walked in. There was a bed, dressing-table and a built-in closet, with another door to the ensuite bathroom — the room was typical of many in the nurses' residence.

The woman tut-tutted at the untidy bed, sweeping up a discarded nightie and putting it under the pillow before he could see it.

Too late.

The carpet under the window by the radiator squelched as she passed it.

'There we are, when you've finished don't forget to check out with me will you?'

He promised he would. When she was gone he set his box down and knelt by the offending radiator. It was a ten-minute job, but when he left he would give her a bit of blarney about needing time to let the resin bonding dry. Whilst his hands were clean he had other things to do.

Nieminen took the nightie from under the pillow, ran its nylon through his hands, held it close to his face. It smelt of woman. He put it back, and turned his attention to the dressing-table.

Nieminen lifted up the framed picture of the girl, was delighted to find she was a peach — it made it all the better. He pulled the top drawer open. It was full of jewellery. Not interested, he closed it again. Once he'd stolen something and the suspicion and the police investigation had been frightening.

No, what he took now were things which the girls themselves would never be sure where they had lost.

He chuckled at that and found in the second drawer what he was looking for: panties.

This girl favoured lots of colours. He delicately picked up a red pair. Holding them on both sides at the waist, making them twist as if the girl was in them. Nieminen did the same with all of them before he came back to the red ones. His large calloused hand closed over the scrap of nylon and thrust it into his pocket.

He closed that drawer and opened another. It contained slips and nighties; a third had woollens. Nieminen opened the closet, ran a hand along the line of dresses, putting his hand up under the hem, pretending he was groping the girl. He drifted into the bathroom, suddenly thought he heard somebody at the door, and fiddled with the faucets. It was a false alarm.

Nieminen looked at himself in the mirrored cabinet before opening the door. It contained all the usual things — painkillers, indigestion tablets, shampoos, talcum powder and tampons — and tin foil strips containing tablets, which he instantly recognized as the Pill.

He felt he knew the bitch intimately now. His hand strayed to the silky scrap in his pocket, before he commenced work.

He was still feeling them when he left, checking with the woman in the hall and politely taking his leave, all the time with his hand on his trophy.

Tonight he would wear them, his own dark exciting secret.

★ ★ ★

Dr Steven Hacker locked his car in the parking lot next to the tower block that contained his fourth floor Department. He was the specialist in maxillo-facial surgery covering all accidents to the face as well as the recipient of problems sent in by the area's dentists.

That morning was his day for the routine assessment of new cases and he knew that at least twenty people would need to be seen before his O.R. list at noon.

The thought did not help his temper. In the short drive from home the realization that his divorce was about to become public had finally sunk in.

He ran his hands through his blond curly hair, and turned into the entrance hall, eschewing the elevators and with his briefcase creaking and banging against his thigh, took the steps two at a time. Of less than average height, Hacker made up for his short stature with a sturdiness and a fitness that he worked on with pride. His breathing was hardly affected as he reached the double-doors of his department and pushed through.

His mind raced ahead to the clinic he had tonight, and his last 'patient'.

They couldn't be seen together around the hospital, word would soon get around and rumours would be rife. No, they had to play it very carefully.

Hacker did some of his private consultations at a clinic forty miles out of town.

27

There, they would talk in his car, for there was a lot to decide on . . .

Before that, there was something he had to do.

2

Jean Hacker arrived half an hour after her husband, parking her little white compact an eighth of a mile away in the lot reserved for staff of the Emergency Room.

She locked the car up and ran into the department through the ambulance entrance coming face to face with Peter Norris, the Emergency Resident.

'Peter — I'm sorry I'm late.'

Norris waved a hand deprecatingly.

'It's all right — we've not been inundated yet.' They walked together to the staff-room door, where Norris left her, leaving Jean Hacker momentarily looking at his retreating back.

Why hadn't she said something then about why she was late? In the locker-room she changed into her clinical kit, checked the pockets as a matter of routine: stethoscope, bleeper, pens. She shut the door, and then leaned back against the cold metal. She knew why. Steven was on the staff here — she was only in lowly clinical posts. Most of them were men — and Jean was conscious of the feelings she seemed to generate — possibly due to Steven's insidious propaganda. She knew she was reckoned to be a stuck-up bitch.

She walked past the Emergency Room where James Larsson had been received fewer than twelve hours ago. Beyond was a corridor of cubicles where anything from nosebleeds, to gunshot wounds and cardiac arrests were given their initial assessment and treatment. Patients, nurses and students were milling around.

She chalked her name up on the Doctors on Duty Board and faced the senior nurse in her dark blue uniform sitting at a large desk.

'Morning.'

'Morning, Doctor.'

'What have we got then?' The woman handed her a treatment card.

'Cubicle ten. P.U.O. Age six, male.'

Jean started in the direction of her patient, saying almost casually, 'Sorry I'm late, but things came to a head at home — we're divorcing.'

Why she said it then, and to a nurse she was not particularly close to, she had no idea. Maybe she was trying it out — saying it out loud.

'Oh, I'm sorry to hear that.' The woman's voice was not in keeping with the sentiment, more eager to pass on the juicy piece of news. Jean realized that that might be another motive for her impulsive behaviour.

She reached cubicle ten and pulled back the curtain. She was confronted by two students and a nurse gathered around a fierce-looking woman, and a fretful, grubby-faced child who was lying on the couch dressed only in his underpants and socks. Jean drew the curtain behind her.

And so it went on all morning until she found herself at lunch, sitting at the end of the cafeteria reserved for staff, as opposed to the rest of the room without tablecloths where the students came and went in noisy crowds.

'May I join you?'

She looked up, groaned inwardly at the bearish figure towering over her. Charles Seigle set his tray down before she had time to reply — not that she could have been rude anyway.

He spaced out his plates and set aside the tray.

'You look tired, Jean.'

So the strain was showing. She nibbled half-heartedly at some salad.

'Do I?' He dug heartily into his steak as, resignedly, Jean put her fork down and sipped her coffee.

Seigle shovelled the food into his mouth in mammoth forkfuls. They talked for a couple of minutes, until Seigle ended a pause with a sly look.

31

'Have you met Pam Mortimer the new psychiatrist yet?'

Jean set her coffee down.

'No, I haven't.'

Seigle suddenly stood up.

'Well, here's your chance.'

Jean turned to find a woman standing beside her, placing her tray on the table. She held out her hand. Jean took it and they shook as Seigle did the introductions. Pam Mortimer murmured,

'I've heard so much about you — I seem to know you already.'

Jean looked from the woman's face, with its high cheekbones and finely plucked eyebrows crowned by luxuriant raven hair that spread out from a widow's peak, to Charles Seigle.

'Really — from whom?'

Seigle smiled down on her.

'Oh, I've tried to help Pam settle in as quickly as possible — so I've been going through the staff-list.'

Pam Mortimer sat down followed by Seigle as Jean pulled a face.

'I hope what he said was all good.'

The psychiatrist smiled. 'Indeed it was. He said you were beautiful and now I can see why.'

Embarrassed, Jean shot a glance at Charles Seigle, but he was grinning like an idiot. She knew instantly that Pam Mortimer was *different*.

Some subtle inflexion in the way she said beautiful, combined with a fractionally over-intense look, suggested her interest in her own sex.

Seigle did most of the talking, Jean staring fixedly down at her salad, rather than face those dark eyes.

The Pathologist ended with —

'So I'm taking Pam to see Tosca tonight — loads of back-stabbing and emotion — just like this place.' He chuckled at his own joke.

Looking up Jean found herself confronted by the smiling knowing eyes that hinted not of the passion of Tosca, but at a dark female passion, a world without the brute insensitivity of selfish men, more ancient Greek than Roman.

Jean felt the two burning spots on her cheeks as she abruptly got up pushing her chair back and excusing herself.

'I've got to see an extra patient, came in last night in a coma-like state.'

That indeed was true. If anything of exceptional interest was on offer in the hospital, the Medical Institute circulated all department notice boards with details. As it was, Norris had mentioned it to her at coffee that morning.

The expression he'd used was — weird. All the classic signs, sluggish eye reflex, flaccid limbs etc, but not low-blood pressure and no obvious brain damage. From the meagre history it seemed likely to have been an overdose of pentothal.

Her eyebrows had shot up, so he had explained, 'He's been tortured by the Taliban or Al Queda — he was behind enemy lines when he was captured. They were no doubt trying to get information out of him.

'Bit of a hard case to have survived at all. He's a trained killer of course, otherwise he wouldn't be in the Special Forces, would he?'

Jean had given an involuntary shiver.

To Pam Mortimer she said, 'I expect I'll see you again soon.'

It was quite the normal thing one would say out of politeness, but Jean felt that the woman was reading something else into it.

Pam Mortimer said matter of factly —

'I look forward to it.'

As she walked away she was conscious of eyes on her back.

Jean's troubled thoughts were far from the patient she was riding the elevator to see.

It was not everyday that one's marriage finally went on the rocks. That was why, she persuaded herself, she was over-reacting to Pam Mortimer.

And then came the memory of the sudden spasm deep inside her at the woman's look, as though a snake had been sleeping, dormant all her life, and had suddenly moved.

Had she been denying its existence all these years?

Like many girls at a single-sex convent school, she had had a crush on one of the teachers when she was fourteen. Sister Romans had been the biology mistress and had taken a special interest in her.

But there had been no nonsense, for want of a better word, and it had been a day school. Until this moment in her life Jean had never thought of it in any other way. Now, she wondered, was she cold with men — was that the fault at the heart of her marriage?

Feeling wretched she found her way into the Critical Care Unit and checked with the nursing station.

'I'm here to give the once over to . . . ' She searched for the name she had written down.

'James Larsson?' suggested the Staff nurse.

Fumbling still with her papers Jean agreed. 'Yes, that's right.' Staff led the way.

'You must be the fifth doctor we've had up here today. I'm going to ask Sister to arrange a timetable.'

Jean protested.

'Really; if it's too much trouble . . . '

35

Staff shook her head.

'With him, hardly?'

She led the way to a bed in the corner and began pulling the curtain around.

'Could you check out with me when you leave, please?'

'Of course.'

Jean set her things down on the chair to one side and turned to the sheet-covered patient. The badly sutured cheek wound was so vivid against the white background that for a second that's all she was conscious of.

Then her gaze took in the whole of his face. What Jean saw made her totally forget her fear of only seconds before.

He was handsome in a rugged sort of way, and yet that wasn't the thing that really got to her. There was something else, something that made him irresistible.

It was the *vulnerability*. In his coma this tough attractive looking man was as helpless as a newborn child, and they needed a woman to survive.

Jean shook her head as if to bring herself back to reality. Now she *was* convinced of her over-emotional state.

She pulled back the sheet. When she saw what had been done to him her response was involuntary.

'Oh God.'

She spent fifteen minutes examining the patient, lifting each muscled leg and testing for the reflex. When she got to his arms she held each one out straight noting the badly bruised puncture marks where the pentothal, if that's what it was, had been roughly injected.

Whether it had been his struggles or the sheer unprofessionalism of the person with the syringe, but it had been nothing short of a butcher's job.

She ran a hand down to his palms, conscious of their width and the hard, calloused skin — so different from her own — and all the men in her working life. Steven and his colleagues had hands as soft as hers: it went with the job. Jean shivered at the thought of them on her body, and knew in that moment that she wasn't cold with men, it was just that she had never been with anyone as *masculine* as this man.

She finally stood back, appraised the patient lying helplessly before her, naked and wired to the equipment that was monitoring his every function.

Jean whispered — 'What have they done to you?'

She got out her ophthalmoscope and leaned over him, bringing her face right down to his as she sent the beam of light into the black hole that was his pupil.

Jean breathed out in excitement. There *had* been a reaction more than noted in the records, albeit a sluggish one. She pulled back, spoke to him.

'Well done . . . What's your name?'

She turned to the front of the notes.

'*James*. That's a lovely name. Well done, James.'

Jean talked aloud, the better to stimulate the brain.

'If you go on like this we'll soon have you running around. Who's coming to visit you? Are you married?'

She glanced again at the hard looking hands, noting for the second time the toughened skin on the edges. There was no sign of a wedding ring.

Jean shuffled through the notes.

'Strange — you don't seem to have anyone as next of kin.'

She looked once more at the battered face that she found so appealing.

'I'll come every day, all right?'

With no real necessity she checked his pupil reflex again.

There it was.

Delighted Jean Hacker whispered near his ear —

'You're going to be all right, James. I'm so pleased for you.'

On impulse and quite unprofessionally, she kissed his forehead and brushed his hair back with her hand.

'See you tomorrow then.'

Before she left the unit she informed the nurse in charge of his improved eye reflex. She took a last glance across the room to the shape under the sheet in the corner, and then ran lightly down the stairs.

Maybe it was just her feminine psyche fighting back — but she felt a whole lot better.

The third cranial nerve, the occulomotor, which led from James Larsson's brain to his eyeball had reacted. But it was not the only cranial nerve that had fired off impulses. The eighth, the auditory nerve, had recorded the delicate vibrations of his eardrum as it in turn had reacted to her soft husky voice as she talked close to him.

But there was yet another nerve that had reacted even more strongly — the first cranial nerve, the olfactory.

Jean Hacker had chosen to wear a perfume based on oil of roses. And in the deep, dark depths of his tormented mind, James Larsson's last conscious memory was the scent of roses — the scent of the woman who had inflicted so much pain on him.

The brain of James Larsson exploded with

electrical activity. One of the hands that Jean Hacker had held in hers, that had killed a man with a single thrust like an iron ball, began to curl up.

3

Beneath the medical school, in the basement, one hundred new medical students in clean white coats filed apprehensively into the cold, white-tiled dissecting room. Their eyes were drawn to the rows of white mounds on stainless steel tables, the outline of human shapes just caught by the draped sheets.

Somehow that made it worse, their imagination running wild. The demonstrators from the Anatomy Department guided them in groups to the tables. Their dissection of the human animal would take some eighteen months to complete.

The Senior Demonstrator clapped his hands for attention.

'Right, remove the sheets, fold them and place them on the rack beneath the table. They must be used to re-cover the cadaver at the end of each session.'

The sheets were gingerly removed. The rows of bodies were not like most students had imagined they would be. There was no white flesh as in the post-mortem room, no soft pliable tissue.

Instead, the cadavers appeared to be

41

covered by a thick brown, greasy skin. The smell of the preserving fluid was strong. The bodies had only just been removed from their plastic bags in the refrigerated storeroom, where others hung like so many prepacked carcases.

One young bespectacled youth was helped away and shown where the toilet was. The Chief Demonstrator, already overworked, called out irritably —

'Come along now, you've all done dissections at college. This is no different. Now can I see you getting on please? If you have any questions, don't hesitate to ask one of us.'

The six students in the far corner gingerly gathered at the head of their cadaver — soon to be nicknamed 'Bertie'.

They were good, able students and quietly got on cutting and reflecting back the thick brown skin covering the side of the head and neck. It was like cutting into the outer layers of what they imagined a mummy might be like.

★   ★   ★

Dr Steven Hacker operated all afternoon, finishing at four o'clock after two hours of working a difficult reconstruction of a mandible smashed in a road wreck. He was helped out of his gown by a nurse and scrubbed up quickly. In less than fifteen minutes he was in his car and on the way home. Jean would not be leaving the hospital for another hour. That would be all the time he needed. She wouldn't be expecting him back until after his private surgery — about eleven p.m.

Hacker turned into the drive and pulled up at the front door. He went straight in and made for the stairs. Many times over the past few weeks he'd dreamed of this moment, rehearsed it in his imagination. In no time he'd flung the contents of several clothes drawers into his bag and zipped it shut. A second bulging one was soon dumped by the first. In twenty minutes his car was full of clothes, and a cardboard box piled with books.

Satisfied he slammed the door shut. There was just one more thing he had to do: In the drawing-room he found the photograph he wanted.

It was of a young woman sitting on a gate. She was unsophisticated, with a look almost of a blue stocking. Jean MacArthur had just qualified when the photograph had been taken, in the week of their engagement.

Still with his eyes on it he moved into the kitchen and sat down and wrote a terse note to her.

When he'd finished he placed the note by the kettle, and backed away, looking in turn from it to the picture in his hands. They began to shake. Something came over him, the blind rage at the failure of his marriage. It was not his fault.

Suddenly he smashed it on the ground, put his heel on the broken glass and ground it into small pieces.

Leaving the front door wide open he walked out of the house, got into his car and drove away.

The wind played with the leaves in the trees, swung the door gently, emphasizing in the abandonment, that the home was now just a house.

A lonely house.

★ ★ ★

Dr Simon Limbach came down the grand staircase in the main hall of the Medical School. The walls were lined with portraits of Past Presidents of the Medical Society and Deans of the College, staring with stern Victorian fortitude down on the throng of students.

The gap in the technical knowledge between when they were lecturing and now, was enormous, but the ancient volume under

Limbach's arm, written by one of them and which he had been quoting to the students now heading for the bar in their club, was — The Principles and Practice of Medicine'.

It had been written in eighteen-ninety.

Some things never changed.

Limbach nodded at the porter standing behind his counter next to the revolving doors.

Out in the street he bumped into Jean Hacker as she came out of the Emergency Room.

'My dear, how are you?'

Jean was in a hurry to get home. All afternoon she had tried to calm down, think things through. Perhaps she had been hasty with Steven. Maybe they could work something out after all — that her outburst might prove to be a good thing in the long-run. When she saw him later that evening she resolved to try again.

'I'm fine thank you, Simon, and a bit tired. And you?'

'Never better. Off to give Charles a game of squash.'

Jean hesitated on the sidewalk as a car left the parking lot.

'Don't know where you get the energy.'

Limbach took her by the elbow as she stepped forward.

'Blame it on my wife. Jane feeds me well. By the way, are you going to the Hospital Ball?'

He continued to hold her elbow as he shambled along with her down the rows of cars.

'I don't think so, Simon.' His features took on a knowing look.

'How are things with you two?'

'Could be better.'

Limbach clicked his tongue and let go of her elbow.

'If there is anything I can do to help — don't hesitate.'

'Thanks, Simon.'

They reached her car and paused.

He put his arm around her, 'The Principles and Practice of Medicine' digging into the small of her back.

'Jane and I are very fond of you. If you need a place to stay — somebody to talk to — you know where to come.'

With that he gave her a real bear-hug, so much so that she came up on her toes out of her shoes. Jean's hands rested on his upper arms. They felt like iron.

Limbach gave her a kiss on her cheek, very near her mouth, then released her.

'Bye now, see you around.'

Relieved, Jean released the door lock.

Soon she was driving out of the lot, her rear lights and indicator lost in the stream of home bound traffic.

After Jean had left the hospital grounds, the figure who had frozen with shock at the sight of her and Limbach together, had seen what appeared to be a passionate embrace, remained.

In the space of just minutes Marjorie Gooding had been consumed by jealousy — and then rage; in all the time she had worked for Simon he had never once touched her like that.

And with that — *harlot*.

Marjorie Gooding thought about Jean Hacker all the way home. She made her evening meal gazing into the steam rising from her boiling potatoes — the surface a little picture of hell itself. In front of the TV her unseeing eye recorded the drama of NCIS as they unravelled the tangled web of deceit and death in the Navy, but her mind was preoccupied with visions of other deceits.

Of other deaths.

Of one *violent* death.

4

Pam Mortimer lay in her bath, luxuriating in the warm embrace of the water, playing with great lumps of foam. Her hair was tied back, revealing the curve of her neck. She raised her knee, watched the bubbles slide down, followed it with the back of her fingers, satisfied with its smooth, silky feeling.

If — and it was a big if — she allowed Charles Seigle the pleasure of her body he would find everything entirely to his liking.

Pam Mortimer gently held her breasts, pushing them together and upwards, admiring her own cleavage. She smiled. Yes, no doubt those large hands of his would be eager to cup these 'little treasures'. Despite the hot water she gave a little shiver at the thought of those very same hands arranging the limbs of dead women day in and day out.

She knew she had a good body, many a man had said so, but their comments were glib and so obvious as they had sweated and laboured and frequently swore their way to an orgasm over her — never *with* her.

Men were too self-centred, too uncaring. Now a woman — that was different, she *knew* what another woman really felt. Only females had the delicacy, the lightness of touch, the imagination to raise their sisters to heaven.

And Jean Hacker . . .

Pam Mortimer closed her eyes. There could be no doubt that Jean had recognized her interest.

★   ★   ★

They were still warming up, thwacking the ball in a relaxed easy manner, trying shots they wouldn't risk later.

Seigle sported a sweatband around his forehead, his large shoulders swinging easily as he stroked the squash ball back against the wall, watching it rebound high over Simon Limbach until it dropped dead in the corner.

He looked at his watch.

'Let's start, I've got to eat before the opera.'

Limbach retrieved the ball.

'Ah, yes, Doctor Mortimer.' There was an edge to his voice.

Seigle frowned.

'What's wrong with that?'

Limbach bounced the ball at his feet and took up his serving position.

'Nothing — nothing at all.'

Seigle pulled at his sweatband.

'You don't believe all that crap do you? Pam's a good looking woman.'

'Not all lesbians are butch and look like the back of a bus, you know,' snapped Limbach. 'Besides, the bible says that sort of thing is an abomination.'

Seigle suddenly remembered Limbach's religious fervour. The man wasn't being frivolous — he meant every word of it.

He shook his head in disgust.

'Let's get on with the game.'

Seigle guessed who was at the bottom of this latest smear. As he whipped the ball hard with his first stroke, it carried with it all the fury the thought of Jean Hacker evoked.

Again and again the racquet cut the air.

Limbach struggled to contain his furious strokes.

★ ★ ★

Jean turned up the unmade road with its poor nineteen-thirties lighting that really only gave out dull yellow cones of soft light with dark spaces between.

Her headlights picked up the potholes, the gyrating trees in the wind, and finally swept around and up the short drive of the last house standing before the impenetrable blackness of the woods.

There were no inviting lights in the rooms; the house was in complete darkness. She didn't expect Steven to be home of course.

And then she saw the front door, moving back and forth in the eddying wind. Jean slowed, then stopped with the car headlights still pointing at the house, their light carrying part way into the hall revealing the doors to the downstairs rooms.

Fear gripped her. Intruders?

Were they still on the premises? Every woman's nightmare come true.

Jean sat in the car for minutes, undecided. She hadn't been herself that morning; maybe she had left the door like that?

Slowly she eased the car forward, turned it so that it was pointing directly at the door.

Jean left the engine running, got out, and walked hesitantly up to the entrance, calling over her shoulder.

'Steven — have you left the door undone?'

Her voice was tight with fear, not the matter-of-fact sound she had tried to convey in pretence that she was accompanied. The door creaked on its hinges, half-shutting. She pushed it back, stepped inside, her hand darting for the switch. Instantly the hall was lit up in the bright everyday miracle of electricity.

Feeling better, she advanced further and

with a rush reached the kitchen straight ahead.

For a second after she flicked the switch nothing happened, then a flash came as the fluorescent tube flared. In that instant her eyes took in the fact that the room was empty, and that a letter was propped against the kettle. As she walked towards it her shoes trod on the shards of glass.

Slowly Jean bent and retrieved her crumpled photo. Heart sinking, she read the note.

He had gone, moved in with a friend, no address. Any communication was to be through lawyers, the house to be sold and revenue divided.

Jean slumped into a chair, buried her face in her hands and sobbed, uncaring that the wind still played with the open front door, that the car stood with its engine running and its headlights full on.

As she cried for her lost marriage she ignored the fact that an intruder could be in the house.

★ ★ ★

The nursing team had been alerted to the change of state in James Larsson by Jean Hacker, but the next twelve hours were unique in their experience.

His blood pressure began to fluctuate at the same time as movements increased in his limbs, little jerks growing in frequency and strength.

An intern checked his reflexes again.

'Any change at all — page me.'

At three o'clock in the morning James Larsson, already thrashing from side to side, suddenly reared up, mouth open.

The scream came from hell itself echoing down the corridors and ventilation shafts.

Staff rushed from all over the unit to restrain him, fighting to keep the drip in place, and the criss-crossing leads attached to his skull and chest.

'Jesus, hold him down.'

But the sweeping right arm of knotted muscle sent a doctor crashing back into the monitors. Screens exploded in showers of sparks. A burly security guard joined in as two students threw themselves across his body, pinning him down. One of the nurses shouted in his face.

'James: it's all right. Everything's O.K. You're all right. James, listen to me.'

The dishevelled doctor climbed to his feet.

'No good, give me a syringe.'

James Larsson abruptly stopped struggling.

'No. No drugs.'

His voice was hoarse, his throat raw, as though he had screamed for hours, days, on end. Gradually they drew back. The students got off him, released their grip.

The doctor shook his head in disbelief.

'Never seen anything like it. We'll get your case reviewed in the morning.'

They all stood in a semi-circle, gazing at the man who looked back at them from the wreckage of his cubicle.

James Larsson had returned to consciousness, but not to *reality*.

He awaited the *terror*. It came in several forms, but there was one of them in particular — a woman.

He'd smelt the roses.

James Larsson looked around, his senses magnified, knew instantly that she was not there.

Well, he was ready this time.

He smiled back at them.

He could wait.

5

In front of her dressing-table mirror Jean looked back at her face, at the dark rings under her eyes.

She set about trying to correct the worst effects of a night of crying and lack of sleep, finally searching for a couple of pain killers for a splitting headache. The room needed fresh air, so she opened the window. It was a lovely sparkling morning, sunshine streaming into the room. The garden lawn was bright with a greenness that contrasted with the darkness of the wood beyond. Birds chirped and bustled around, flying up and down from the grass to the bushes. She loved that view, but realized that for her it would soon be gone forever. There was no way she could pay off Steven's half — it would have to be sold. Jean resented that.

Last night, what he had done to her photograph had been disturbing. He was clearly not himself. This friend he was staying with had spoken volumes of what had been going on. Jean Hacker had passed through many stages in the wee small hours, but the one that had grown strongest was *resentment*.

In their mailbox was a pile of post, mostly junk, but two of the letters were for Steven.

As Jean crunched over the gravel to her car, she remembered that she had no forwarding address for this *friend's* house. She would have to point this out to him. It would be interesting to see where he had shacked up, and more importantly, with *whom*. Her car roared away, leaving the house to settle into the emptiness of the day.

The bedroom window above the kitchen extension remained open.

★ ★ ★

George Nieminen punched his card and put it back into the rack, then turned along the corridor into the office. His boss was sitting there scratching his chin, collar open, newspaper laid out on the desk before him.

He looked up as Nieminen entered.

'There's an urgent job in D12 — the ventilation system.'

Nieminen grunted, quite happy to get on with the job.

Last night had been great. His new found friend had admired his latest acquisition from the nurses' room and it had all gone on from there.

His journey in the tunnel took him to the

stairs that led up to the medical school. He passed them, went on along the white-tiled route lit only by occasional strip-lights.

This was the worst part of the job as far as he was concerned. He was very near to the place where they stored the bodies for the students to cut up. The air was cold and smelt of disinfectant and formaldehyde.

He hurried on, happy to turn left and into the section that led to the hospital and the large storerooms for the pharmacy that was D12.

The metal-frame shelves ran in long corridors, reaching to the roof. Cardboard cartons and carboys, jars and plastic bags filled the available area. He found the ware-house foreman who took him to the faulty ventilation outlet.

'I'll leave you to it then.'

Nieminen used his electric screwdriver and took off the three by four foot grille in the wall. In the large horizontal conduit before him that carried power cables as well as ducted air there was an electric circuit box. He began to work on it.

Suddenly a giggle echoed down the metallic corridor, followed by a clanging that he recognized as locker doors slamming. It had never happened before.

He froze, listening to women's voices,

rising and falling, and realized the source was to the right. In his head he worked out the next destination of the system: The sound was emanating from the changing room of the female surgical staff.

He felt the blood surge in his temple. What if he . . .

Nieminen undid his trainers, pulled them off, and then got his head and shoulders into the shaft. It was surprisingly easy. On his stomach, using his elbows, he pulled himself along.

The volume of the voices increased, emanating from a grille only twenty feet away.

A door slammed. He slowed, made sure he was making no sound and then inched his way forward until he could put his eyes to the slats. George Nieminen recoiled with the shock, nearly giving himself away as he hit his head on the metal roof.

A young woman was right there, just below him dressed only in white bra and panties. He recognized her as one of the ER nurses. She turned, seemed to be looking straight up at him, frowning. Nieminen tensed, expecting her to scream out, but she turned away. He could see everything as she prepared for her stint in surgery. When she finally left he relaxed, lay flat on his back, sweating with excitement. The same ducted air-conditioning system ran throughout the hospital, including all the changing-rooms. Nieminen sniggered with delight, at the realization that he could see into almost everywhere.

He sucked in his breath as he suddenly remembered the good-looking ones he could now catch prancing about in their panties.

And one in particular.

Doctor Jean Hacker.

He actually licked his lips as he imagined her.

Jesus, he might even take a photograph. He knew somebody who would pay well for one of that bitch.

*   *   *

James Larsson watched as the nurses bustled around, busy with their morning duties. He was waiting, waiting for the next move *they* would make against him.

He tried to remember how long ago it was since they'd taken him prisoner.

Larsson's team had been ordered out, their job of gathering intelligence in a far remote valley compromised, when, against orders, he'd taken a personal decision to stay.

His comrades had been staggered, but others had guessed it was a death wish.

His wife had been murdered in New York

six months previously.

But things hadn't worked out as he imagined. A week later he'd been cornered as he'd hurriedly sent the co-ordinates for an attack by a drone. After a half-day fire fight with the Taliban, he had been knocked out by a mortar blast.

He had come round a prisoner, and his torment at the hands of his captors — especially the woman in the black burka who smelled of roses — had begun.

Now he flitted between worlds, the world outside his skull, and the turbulent nightmare within. And the two sometimes merged, where reality and fantasy were as one.

A nurse came over to him.

'Ready for a shower, James?'

He smiled. They never gave up. But there was no danger. The air was clean. Not a trace of the scent of roses.

She was not there, the succubus, the She-Devil.

6

Jean Hacker did not call Steven immediately, waiting until there was a break and a cup of coffee. She took herself off down to the phone in the nursing director's office, and rang his extension from there.

'I'd like to speak to Dr Hacker please — this is his wife.'

The voice of the staff nurse on the other end of the line seemed knowing, or was it her imagination?

'Of course. He's just finished his list — can you hold for a moment?'

Jean nodded at the wall chart for diabetics before her and said, 'Yes.'

It seemed to be a long time. Was he being deliberately difficult? Then —

'Hello Jean.'

The normality of his voice was off-putting.

Bitterly she asked, 'The photo, do you hate me that much?'

'It was an accident.'

Unseen, she shook her head in disbelief.

'Did you have to leave like that?'

His voice remained even.

'I think it was for the best.'

Resignedly she asked, 'Where are you staying?'

Without any trace of aggressiveness he replied, 'What does it matter to you?'

She shrugged at the wall chart.

'Well — if for no other reason than forwarding your mail.'

'Send it to the Department.'

Jean was suspicious.

'All right — suit yourself. But why so secretive? I presume there *is* another woman?'

He sounded as reasonable as ever.

'Presume what you like — but don't judge others by your own standards. I would remind you that it was you who asked for the divorce.'

Jean took a deep breath, held it for a few seconds.

'Steven, let's keep this amicable — OK. What do you want me to do about the house?'

'Put it on the market as we said.'

He gave a chuckle.

'Meanwhile, you can have your fancy men back there now.'

Some two months ago when he had refused to accompany her to a drug-company reception she had gone on her own. Nothing untoward happened, but there was always malicious gossip in any small town — which is what the hospital was.

Resignedly she sighed.

'There is no one else, Steven, but let's not argue about that again.'

She couldn't see it, but he smiled as he said, 'If that's all, I must go now, I've got things to do.'

'Yes, that's all, for *now*,' she added with emphasis.

The phone went dead. She looked at the receiver for several seconds before replacing it on its cradle. There was something going on.

Steven had found himself somebody else; she could sense the difference in him. Whoever it was, they were directing events, telling him what to do and how to react.

As she walked back to the main area of the department Jean suddenly felt vulnerable.

There were *two* of them, only one of her.

Vulnerable, and lonely.

★   ★   ★

James Larsson went through some more vigorous tests — physical ones as well as a fresh MRI scan.

'Remarkable' was the word the neurosurgeon used to his little group of students as they talked out of earshot about their patient. He went on, steepling the fingers of his hands together as he thought out loud. 'I think here we are dealing with a case of many layers. He was in a form of unconsciousness when admitted — the pentothal-induced coma, if that is what it was. He has quite exceptional physical toughness which, despite the other injuries he has received, has enabled him to surface very quickly. As you can see the physical signs are encouraging indeed, that's not the problem now. But I think we've got to be careful here not to miss anything.

'I have a feeling that his memory centre in the hippocampus has been damaged by the drugs — we will never know what they were. So I shall refer him to the Department of Psychology for further evaluation.'

He turned back to his patient.

'Major Larsson, you've made very good progress, but there are a couple of things we want to check on — make sure you return to full health. I'd like you to see a colleague of mine — just to make sure we've covered everything.'

Larsson sat on the edge of his bed.

'I'd like to leave now, I feel good.'

The neurosurgeon was taken aback.

'Well now — that's pushing things a bit. I'd say it would be more likely to be a week.'

Larsson raised an eyebrow.

'What's the problem?'

The doctor hesitated, carefully measured his words.

'You had some sort of total withdrawal from reality — it wasn't a coma, but an unconscious state like it. So we've got to make sure the old brain is working again correctly.'

Larsson stiffened, but the doctor seemed not to notice.

'We need to transfer you to the Neller Wing — its much more like a hotel. As long as you do not leave the hospital area you can come and go as you please, watch TV and so on. It's secure at night — essential for some I'm afraid.'

He moved to the window, nodded.

'It's that block there — set in the grounds. It will only be a week. All right?'

The neurosurgeon turned and suddenly found himself looking into eyes that were like the black holes at the end of a shotgun barrel.

Involuntarily he stepped back as Larsson said softly,

'You're saying I'm mad?'

The neurosurgeon thought there was a strong possibility that his colleagues in Neller Wing would find James Larsson *disturbed*, to say the least.

'No, of course not.'

He was annoyed to find his voice had gone up slightly.

'I can assure you that there is no physical damage to your brain, the catscan was clear, but you know yourself that you lost consciousness for several days . . . Better we get to the bottom of it now than let you go prematurely, only to have you blacking out again.'

The figure before him was motionless. Unknown to the neurosurgeon he was smelling the air. She wasn't there.

'I want to speak to the woman doctor.'

The neurosurgeon was puzzled.

He turned to the Sister.

'Do you know to whom he is referring?'

The nurse pulled a face.

'We've had a good few around, but I think it must be Dr Jean Hacker, sir, from the Emergency Room. She came up the other afternoon and detected the first signs of improvement.'

'I see. Have her paged would you, I'll speak to her if it's possible.'

He turned back to Larsson.

'Is there a special reason for you requesting this particular member of staff?'

Larsson smiled. It was unnerving. 'No.'

The neurosurgeon had a busy round to get on with.

'I'll see she comes to you before we make any decision, OK?'

He did not wait for a reply, abruptly closing the medical notes and handing them to his Intern who was pushing the document cart.

The group moved on, leaving Larsson utterly motionless.

So, her name was Doctor Hacker — Jean Hacker.

He savoured it, rolling it around his mouth like a physical entity.

Jean.

Hand-maiden of the devil.

His knuckles turned white as he held onto the end of the bed.

★   ★   ★

Marjorie Gooding had slept for only two hours, and even then they had been only extensions of her fevered restless state.

How could Simon, a God-fearing man, behave like that, and with that woman of all people?

Around six o'clock in the morning she had had a shower, and then sat in front of her dressing-table. If he wanted a woman to look like a whore, then she would damn well play him at his own game.

Marjorie had begun to work on her hair, sweeping it down in a provocative curl near the corner of her mouth. She had seen the style on a poster for a video.

When she was satisfied she pinned it back, and began to work on her face, applying liberal quantities of foundation, blusher and eyeliner.

Finally she'd reached for a lipstick. Not her usual shade, but one she had once been given as a free sample; it produced large, red, glossy lips. With her hair back in place she surveyed the final effect, and had trembled with excitement, hardly able to control herself.

She'd turned to one side; let her robe fall off one shoulder. The wantonness of it all was too much. Once she'd won him over, Marjorie knew she could lead Simon Limbach back to the path of righteousness. Men, they were all the same really. More like boys — dirty little boys: even the ones close to the angels.

And in return she would have her rightful position in society. Maybe the Hacker woman had done her a favour, in a roundabout way. She never gave a thought to the fact that Simon Limbach was married.

Now she sat at her desk, looked once more at her watch. He was late. She pulled at her short skirt, it was riding up again.

Marjorie was aware of the looks she was receiving, and even a whistle as she came down University Street. But she hadn't heard the sniggering.

About the same time as Jean Hacker's bleeper was emitting its plaintive call, Simon Limbach entered the secretaries' floor, and approached her desk. His mouth opened in amazement.

'Good God, what have you done to yourself?'

She smiled coyly up at him.

'What do you mean?'

He gestured at her.

'All the paintwork.'

This time she did hear a giggle. A little bead of doubt suddenly found life at the back of her mind.

'I . . . I'm going out tonight.'

Limbach frowned, put the records he was holding down on her desk and said sourly,

'Where to — a truckers' stop-over?'

Nearby a couple of girls sniggered.

The doubt mushroomed, seized her like an alien thing from within. She felt physically sick. He was laughing at her, they were all laughing at her.

'Simon, I don't think that's very funny.'

He patted her shoulder.

'Marjorie my dear, I didn't mean to hurt you. It's just that you don't normally dress so . . . how shall I put it . . . *provocatively*. Modesty becomes a woman, as Our Lord . . . '

The thing inside released an acid that

burnt into her gut. Marjorie Gooding leapt up from her chair, brushed past him, upsetting the folders that fell to the floor, and ran for the door to the ladies rest room.

Inside, she locked herself in a cubicle and opened her mouth as the alien thing that was burning her insides leapt out, splattering the lavatory bowl.

* * *

Charles Seigle finished his lecture on the pathology of the thyroid gland, and turned off the laptop that had been in use for his slide show.

'There you are,' his voice was full of sarcasm as he looked around, 'now you know all there is to know about what can go wrong with this important gland — remember that when you're buying me a scotch — and make it a double.'

There was a ripple of laughter.

Seigle placed some papers back into a folder, put his textbooks on top, and dismantled the laptop connections.

Out of the corner of his eye he saw the two very tasty looking girl students he'd noticed before, moving towards him, picking their way down the steep steps of the lecture room.

He hung back, pretending to shuffle some

papers; he knew that these girls wanted to impress, get their faces well known to the academic staff in an effort to promote their grades. And when hospital appointments were being handed out . . . He'd seen it all before.

But these two were *different*. One was a dark haired girl with fine features — possibly with a touch of the Chinese, the other, a large healthy, busty girl.

He had seen them before, and had heard rumours. *Exciting* rumours.

'Dr Seigle — could you spare a moment?'

He looked up, pretending surprise.

'Yes — of course.'

The busty one had spoken first, but the darker girl now asked,

'We didn't quite understand the chemical changes.'

He smiled.

'I don't suppose half the class did — but at least you admit it. Would you like me to go through it with you?'

The girls flashed looks at each other.

'We need to get to the next lecture, we won't be free until well after five.'

He pretended to think, then held his breath as he said —

'Would you like to come to my office at say, six o'clock?'

71

The girls looked at each other, this time quite openly. At six it would be getting dark, the school quite empty.

They nodded at each other. Both knew his reputation, and had decided that rather than fool around any more with their peers, who in any case always wanted to get emotionally involved, they would target the staff, anyone who could help with their careers.

'That's very kind of you, we'll be there at six then.'

They walked away, Annabel making sure that he could see the rolling movement of her gluteal maximus.

Seigle smirked with pleasure.

He knew their game, and he was willing to play it. The thyroid might be what they would initially talk about, and look at stained sections, but just by 'accident' the specimen male organ, caught in all its glorious arousal, sealed forever in a large jar, would be on his desk.

That ought to push things along a little.

He hummed aloud as he passed quickly down through the tunnel, not noticing the strong smell of formaldehyde as he passed the dissecting rooms closed doors.

As the old saying went, people who worked in breweries couldn't smell the hops.

* ★ ★

Jean took the elevator, puzzled by the phone message from the nurse that the neurosurgeon wanted to see her.

She stepped out as the doors parted and very nearly collided with him as he stood with his entourage.

'Ah, Dr Hacker.'

He drew her aside.

'That extraordinary fellow in the coma — Larsson.'

Her heart leapt.

'Is he all right?'

He raised his eyebrows questioningly at her anxiety.

'As regards the coma, yes, he's out of it, but I want him over at Psychological Medicine *now*. He's not happy about it and wants to discuss it with you.'

'Me?' She was startled.

'Yes — you. See if you can persuade him. He doesn't seem to understand that I will get a court order if necessary. I'm very concerned about his condition.'

The entourage crowded into the elevator around him. As the doors closed his last words were,

'The man's a walking time-bomb.'

Shocked, Jean hurried into the unit, and

saw that his bed was empty. She turned to look for a nurse and gave a little gasp.

Towering over her was the man she had only ever seen as a sheet covered body on a gurney, and his eyes were boring into her with unwavering intensity.

7

'Oh.' Jean stepped back, stammered — 'I'm glad to see you've recovered. You wanted to see *me*?'

'Yes.'

She picked up his records and moved nearer to the window.

'Why *me*?'

He slumped down onto the end of the bed and seemed to have lost his strength. Finally he looked up at her, and smiled. It was extraordinary, as if sunlight had spread across a bleak hillside.

'Because you smell of roses.'

Jean's hand went instinctively to her neck where she had put the scent.

She grinned in turn, realizing what must have happened.

'I see — it came through to you while you were asleep?'

He nodded.

She knew that the olefactory nerve was one of the last to succumb in a coma.

Jean took a second or two before she asked shyly,

'So what can I do for you?'

'They want me to move to another department, where the shrinks can get at me.'

Jean leaned back against a radiator.

'And you don't want to go?'

'I feel — O.K.'

Thinking, she played with the stethoscope in her pocket.

'You know about *shrinks*? You've seen them before?'

He remembered the vigorous selection board for the Special Forces.

'Maybe. Anyway I feel very fit.'

Jean Hacker took the stethoscope out of her pocket and clamped it around her neck.

'Let me just check a couple of things, for my own benefit. Roll up your sleeve.'

He did as he was told, watching as she felt for his pulse with cool slim fingers.

She was so beautiful — his heart ached.

How could so much evil lie behind that glorious face, within that delicate body? And there was something else about her that he was struggling with . . .

She finally released his wrist, and reached for the manometer and began wrapping the rubber cuff around his arm.

Nothing was said, but she was conscious of being closely observed.

The python-like grip of the cuff came on as she pumped in air, bled it out, and repeated the process, listening with the stethoscope for the released systolic and diastolic rush of blood in his arteries. Finally she unclipped the stethoscope from her ears and unwound the rubber.

'Quite amazing. You'll do very well, Major Larsson.'

He smiled again, his eyes softening.

'Call me James.'

Jean felt a warmness — recognized it for what it was; she had never denied to herself that she had found him attractive.

'All right,' she said softly.

Jean took the stethoscope from around her neck, played with it in a futile gesture she realized was an attempt to try to erect a professional barrier between them, and spoilt it immediately as she said,

'I'm Jean.'

'I know.'

'You do — how?'

She tried to see her nametag, unable to recall if it said Dr J. Hacker or Dr Jean Hacker.

'I heard the doctor call you that.'

Jean inclined her head.

'I see. You don't miss much do you?'

He said nothing, seemed again to be weak, and hung his head.

Anxiously she asked,

'How do you think I can help?'

His mouth tightened.

'You came to see me, you spoke — remember?'

Jean felt her cheeks burning. Had he also remembered the kiss on the forehead? She cleared her throat.

'Yes. So, what's the problem?'

Larsson gestured with his hand at the wall.

'I want out, away from this place. Can you help me?'

Her face must have fallen because he added quickly —

'I don't mean that I'm not grateful for all that you have done, *Jean*.'

It was the first time he had used her name.

Blushing, she turned to the window, looked out across the grounds, then to the rooftops of the city beyond. Silhouetted on the horizon she could see the woods on the hills that ran down to their house.

Theirs?

No more.

She turned back.

'Look, if you move from here now, to the Neller Wing for twenty-four hours, I'll see what I can do to get you a place to stay for the rest of the treatment — O.K?'

James Larsson turned to face her.

'You'd really do that, for me?'

She spread her hands.

'I can't promise anything, of course.'

There was a pause before he asked softly, 'Why?'

She looked blankly back.

'What do you mean, 'why'?'

'Why would you do that, go to all that trouble?'

For the first time since he'd regained consciousness, she used his name aloud.

'James, you asked for me, don't forget, and I'm afraid of the consequences if you don't get treatment. You're in post-traumatic shock.'

'Ah, yes, the consequences.'

Jean knew that she wasn't being completely honest either with him, or herself.

When he didn't say anything else she added hastily,

'So — will you do it . . . for *me*?'

James Larsson smiled, warmly, knowingly.

'In that case, of course.'

This was the bit outside his skull. Inside he could smell roses . . . roses that would die.

8

It had been a long hard day. Jean's limbs felt heavy as she turned the car into the drive and stopped outside the front door. The sun had already set, the dark forest looming all around the house.

Her steps crunched on the gravel, punctuating the sound of the rustling leaves. Jean fitted the key into the door and entered. As soon as it closed behind her it shut out all the noise of the outside world, leaving only the steady deep clonking of the grandfather clock in the gloom.

She made a cup of coffee and, kicking off her shoes, sank into a favourite old wicker chair. The first sip of the hot liquid was gorgeous — helped her to relax and think about the day.

Her face clouded. She'd spent the last hour at the hospital trying to keep her promise to James Larsson, phoning through the list of landladies the Social Services had supplied.

Once they heard he was in Neller Wing undergoing tests they were suddenly full up or redecorating. What she was going to do when she met him tomorrow she did not know. But there was no way she would let him down.

Jean set the empty cup on a work surface, collected her shoes, and made her way up the staircase, intent on a hot bath. She passed the large landing window, unbuttoning her dress and entered the dark bedroom. Still walking, Jean let the dress fall and stepped from it, before switching on the light on the dressing-table.

Turning, she picked it up, put it on the hanger that she had left on the bed, and opened one of the fitted closet doors.

After hanging it up she looked at herself in the long mirror on the inside of the door.

Jean ran her hands down her satin slip, stretching it over her hips, swung sideways, looking at herself at that angle, then the other.

She was still slim, thanks to summer tennis and winter badminton. Jean ran the back of her fingers under her chin. The skin was firm.

The bedside phone emitted its shrill imperative.

Startled, Jean lay down across the bed to reach it.

'Jean Hacker.'

'Hello Jean, it's Pam.'

Her voice was low, intimate. Jean felt herself blushing, as if Pam were in the room with her, and could see her as she was.

'Pam, what do you want?'

There was a pause for a couple of seconds that seemed to go on for ever, then —

'It's about James.'

Jean was taken aback.

'James?'

'Yes, James Larsson — the patient referred to us — I believe you have an interest?'

'Yes that's right. I've been trying to get him accommodation for the coming week.'

'Any luck?'

'No — it's much more difficult than I imagined.'

'I could have warned you of that. Look, he is coming here tonight, then I'm seeing him tomorrow for a first assessment, can I meet you for coffee?'

'Why — what do you want to discuss?'

'Well, if you haven't got anywhere with finding him somewhere I might need your help to persuade him that it's in his best interests to stay where he is.'

'I see. Well, of course — if I can help in any way.'

'Good. You're on day-case anesthetics tomorrow, is that right?'

It was true, Jean had a clinical attachment stand-in for one of the anesthesiologists who lectured from eleven o'clock onwards, but there was no reason for Pam Mortimer to know about that — unless she'd made enquiries.

'Yes, I can manage anytime up to 10.30.'

'Good. I'm seeing James at nine o'clock — how about my office at ten? I'll have finished my preliminary work-up by then.'

'Very well.'

They said goodbye.

Jean stood up and turned for the en-suite bathroom. As she did so something made her look to the door across the dark landing. A scratching sound.

It came from Steven's room. Jean experienced a sudden twinge of unease. She moved silently across the carpet, put her hand on the door — hesitated. It came again the distinct noise of something — *somebody* scrabbling around.

An intruder?

Then it hit hard. Steven was back, and being a bastard.

She flung open the door.

The room was empty, the light was on — the window *open*.

Nervously she moved to it and the wild, cold blackness beyond. Jean could not remember leaving it like that.

She reached out to draw the window shut. Just as she touched the frame, out of the blackness came a shape, clawing and hissing for her.

Jean jumped back with a yell. In the swirl of wind and rain the leafy tree branch dipped and writhed, scratching at the glass and woodwork.

Jean saw what it was, got to the wildly banging window, and slammed it shut.

In the silence she began to shake.

Perhaps it would be better if the house sold quickly; it was too big and lonely for her on her own, especially in the emotional state she was in.

★   ★   ★

Steven Hacker unlocked his car door and slid into the front seat of his BMW, tossing his sports bag onto the passenger seat. Twice a week he had a keep-fit session.

He slammed the lever into drive and let the automatic gearbox do the work as he gunned the engine. He thought of his lover and the plans they had made. But the suppressed anger at Jean started to spill out, spoiling his thoughts. At the gym he pumped the bodybuilding machine, grunting in explosive bursts through gritted teeth.

'Bitch Bitch Bitch . . . '

Sweat trickled down his face, neck and

chest. At the fiftieth push up, he held the weights for a second, before lowering them gently onto the rests.

For a few moments he lay still, letting his breathing and heart rate settle before he got up.

In the changing rooms he stripped off his sweat-soaked singlet and shorts, and made his way to the communal showers. The air was filled with steam as he stepped under the spray, spinning the wheel to cold.

Steven Hacker turned slowly around, letting the freezing water course down his spine. When he'd turned full circle he re-adjusted the mix, began shampooing his blond hair.

He spent another few minutes soaping generally and then stood with his back to the spray. Through the steam he found the eyes of a young man, a bar of soap in one hand, moving it slowly over his shoulder and neck.

They were alone when Steven Hacker turned off his water, stepped out, and began towelling himself. He watched as the youth turned letting the water trickle over his body, showing every angle to him.

Finally the youth finished and stepped out. Steven Hacker smiled, but made no attempt, as he would have once, to take it any further. He was happy now, had been for some time.

Simon Limbach took the weekly prayer and bible meeting he organized, not in the chapel where people, distressed about loved ones in the hospital were to be found, but in one of the small lecture rooms.

The assembled worshippers included several nurses, a couple of his patients, and a majority of students, some of the latter with the same intention as the two girls targeting Seigle, only doing it their way.

He frowned at his watch as a student with large glasses took her seat.

It was more than time to start, in fact he was late — something he detested.

But there was no sign of Marjorie. It was upsetting, since she was always exactly on time. She knew how he felt about punctuality.

Limbach, opened his bible at the marker. He knew that some people were uncomfortable about a surgeon being a lay-preacher even though there were more around than they suspected. It was as if their obvious, direct reliance on their Maker somehow detracted from their medical skills.

Limbach though, had no doubts about the constant war between good and evil, between His Maker, and the Devil.

Because the Devil had once been in him,

had caused him to do evil things. Things with women.

No, the Devil and all his works had to be challenged every day, every night.

Still no Marjorie.

He looked around at the assembled group.

'I think we'll begin. The reading tonight is from Exodus Chapter 22, verse 18.'

★　★　★

Nieminen had waited until his shift had finished, and then left with one of the other engineers, but instead of going home he had taken a tool box from the trunk of his car then re-entered the hospital via another route, going to a laundry-room that he had noted during the day.

Now he was already in the air vent, moving rapidly, camera in hand as he pushed along, going much faster than his first tentative entry into this, his private world.

The route he'd chosen was longer than necessary, but straighter, and took him along the line of offices bordering the medical school complex.

Most were now empty and dark — just the odd one lit — with a member of the teaching staff poring over a book.

It was as he was passing a darkened one that he heard the noise: Nieminen froze, scalp tingling.

It came again, a low moaning, like an animal in pain.

Nieminen cringed. Was it some awful experiment? In the physiology Department of the Medical School, he'd seen dogs splayed out on boards, with rotating drums with graphs recording details from electrical leads attached to their surgically opened hearts and lungs.

The moan came again, and with it a low grunt . . . and then a *giggle*.

Nieminen pressed his face to the grille and tried to pick out the vague shapes.

And then he saw — saw the pale smooth body of a naked woman sitting astride the darker shape of a man lying on his back, she was riding him like a trotting horse. Beside them knelt another woman. She had nothing on above the waist, her breasts dangling in the face of the man.

The skin of Nieminen's face bulged into the slats of the grille as he strained to see everything and above all to see who it was.

In his hand was the camera, loaded with extra fast film, good enough for the well-lit changing-rooms he had been making for.

But here?

He wondered about using the flash — they wouldn't know where it came from — would they?

Nieminen was excited, and not just by what he saw.

He saw money and favours; blackmail was not a word that he cared to use.

Suddenly the girl on top lifted back her head, her breath coming in short staccato screams. The man reared up as she climaxed and wrapped his huge hairy arms around her waist, pumping her up and down as he forced her on until he too reached his end.

The girl flopped aside, exposing the man's face for the first time.

Instantly Nieminen recognized the features of Doctor Charles Seigle.

He took his photograph. There was a flash that blinded him, and then all hell broke out.

Seigle pushed the girl aside, but Nieminen was already dragging himself back at high speed in the direction of the storeroom.

Seigle leapt up and rushed for the wall.

There was nothing, no holes, no large pieces of equipment for anybody to hide behind. His eyes went higher, saw the grille and realized it had come from there.

Swearing, he struggled into his underpants; found his trousers as the girls scrambled about pulling on jeans, bras and T-shirts.

'Stay here,' he snapped.

He ran down the corridor in his bare feet, throwing open doors.

The instant he saw the dark square window in the concrete with no grille, he knew it had to be the right place.

Seigle ran over; he thrust his head and shoulders into the darkness. For a moment he saw nothing, then realized with a shock that there was somebody right beside him in the blackness.

The blow hit the side of his head and his world exploded into brilliant light.

It took several seconds before the pathologist came to and groggily got to his feet.

Seigle ran a hand gingerly over his head wincing, but he remembered seeing a toolbox which was now gone, only a screwdriver remained. He picked it up. Under his breath he said,

'Bastard. I'll get you.'

★   ★   ★

It was dark by the time James Larsson followed the porter into the elevator and down to the first floor. He went out onto the main concourse, passing the mass of blue and white direction boards that attested of the diversity of modern medical disciplines.

The porter led him down a short ramp and pushed through a double door — out into the open air. Larsson took a deep breath.

'You all right?' asked the porter.

Larsson smiled, said quietly. 'Yes, everything's fine — now.'

They moved along the tarmac path that ran through some trees and bushes, emerging at a two-storeyed modern building. Larsson glanced up at the sign above the entrance,

Department of Psychological Medicine

Inside was a small reception area. A woman was just putting on her coat as the porter put Larsson's notes on the counter before her.

'This gentleman is from neurology — I believe you're expecting him?'

The woman was clearly impatient.

'You can go straight in — that door there. Take your notes would you?'

He did as he was told, read the sign on the door, then knocked.

Dr Pam Mortimer MD
Consultant Psychotherapist

He heard a woman's voice say, 'Come in'.

Larsson grasped the handle and opened it. Rising from behind a desk was a striking dark-haired woman in her mid-thirties, holding out her hand.

'Major Larsson.'

She was dressed in a dark-green silk blouse, wide belt and tight black skirt.

He took her outstretched hand as she came around the desk and relieved him of his documents.

'Right then, let's see what we've got here. Do sit down.'

She returned to her chair as Larsson sat opposite, watching her as she read through his notes.

Finally she looked up at him, rather oddly.

'I see Doctor Hacker has been involved in your treatment.'

As it didn't seem to require any answer he didn't say anything. She turned a page.

'How did you find her?'

Puzzled he asked,

'How do you mean?'

Pam Mortimer read on, turned another page before answering.

'Well, did you find she was sympathetic — understanding?'

Larsson pretended to consider the matter.

'Yes — she's been very helpful.'

'Good, good.'

She tossed the notes onto the desk and sat back.

'We'll start with a session tomorrow after you've had a good night's sleep. I'll arrange for something if you need it?'

He shook his head.

'No thank you.'

'You'll find the rooms here are just like a hotel.'

He smiled politely.

'Sounds nice after the hospital.'

She sat forward, elbows onto the desk.

'Indeed, but I see Jean is trying to get you an address to stay at, correct?'

'Yes.'

'Why is that?'

Larsson's nostrils flared as he looked around, noting the absence of a window.

'I need to get away from places like this.'

Puzzled, she put her head on one side.

'How do you mean?'

He didn't answer, just shrugged.

Pam Mortimer digested the fact, made a note on his file.

'Are there any questions you'd like to ask me?'

He said, 'Can I go outside when I feel like it?'

She smiled and stood up, walking around the desk.

'Tomorrow. Come along, I'll show you to your room.'

He followed her out into reception. A uniformed man with the flashes of a security company on his shoulder was just settling in behind a desk with a bank of CCTV monitors. A wall mounted TV set was on showing the early evening news.

Pam Mortimer leaned across the reception counter, reaching for a key.

There was no doubt that the doctor's figure was as stunning as the rest of her. Slim legs sheathed in dark nylon were further divided by a fine seam that ran from the heel of her shiny court shoes, up the gently swelling thigh and finally out of sight under the straight black border of her skirt. Larsson guessed she was wearing a belt and stockings, and that she was displaying herself deliberately. He now knew that while Jean Hacker was the one he would finally have to face, this woman was also part of the torture team. And females were the worst, could literally work themselves up into a blood frenzy. It was as if they lacked the constraints that men grew up with or were built into them biologically. There had been one like that in Afghanistan.

The Taliban had found it doubly amusing — his being tortured by a woman, because in their world a woman was inferior to a man, almost worthless in fact.

That was why it had been so extraordinary — because she had been the one in charge. And there had been something else about her . . . something even more extraordinary, and *sinister*.

But this woman was not the one.

She had smelt of roses.

As did Dr Jean Hacker.

He shivered as she straightened and

turned. The woman grinned and pushed down her skirt with the palms of her hands.

'Right, let's get you settled in.'

The room she led him into was functional, with a bed, built-in closet, dressing-table unit with TV and a tight little bathroom.

He looked around, checking out the possibilities of escape.

Pam Mortimer turned.

'I'll see you tomorrow morning then Major.'

Larsson smiled.

'Thank you.'

She paused at the door.

'We're more informal here — call me Pam.'

He carried on smiling.

'Pam.'

'Goodnight James.'

She closed the door.

Larsson, sweating, sat down.

It was some minutes before he began to evaluate his surroundings, and only a few more before he realized how easy it would be to escape.

9

James Larsson had been half-asleep at the foot of a tree when the baying of hunting dogs had brought him to full alert.

He only moved his eyes as he checked the immediate surroundings, then he rolled slowly onto his belly and looked around the trunk. The dogs would not be just ordinary animals trained to find. When they did so they would also kill, conditioned to go crazy on the smell of human blood and offal.

Then he saw them, across the far side of the wooded glade, a whole team making a sweep.

If he stayed where he was he'd be discovered and would have to fight.

His hand held the knife he would use, thrusting at exposed bellies as they leapt, or into eye sockets if they took hold. But he knew they would get him in the end by sheer weight of numbers. And if they didn't, the heavily armed men would. He withdrew further into the trees and knew he'd have to put off his escape for now — for now . . .

He came back to reality in his bed, his sweat stained face caught in the soft light of the twenty-four-hour lamps set in the wall above, as the eyepiece in his door was suddenly filled with a huge pupil.

It stared in for several seconds before the screen came down and blocked it from view.

Still in his own world, Larsson drifted off again into half-consciousness, his hand still holding the knife under the covers.

Only it wasn't a knife — it was a screwdriver he'd found that morning.

Not that it made any difference.

If his intent was deadly, that would be the result.

★   ★   ★

Jean knew that something awful had happened as soon as she entered the car lot. Across by the door of the nurses' home two uniformed police officers were standing guard.

Others stood in a group to one side of the tower block, on the grass. Police tape cordoned off the area. Several nurses on their way to and from the hospital looked on at the scene with pale, drawn faces.

With a sinking feeling, Jean guessed what it meant.

She hurried into the hospital, met a nurse she knew.

Jean jerked her head outside, re-adjusted her shoulder bag.

'What are the police doing out there?'

'You haven't heard?'

Impatiently Jean shook her head.

'No.'

The woman moved nearer, as if afraid of hearing her own voice saying it out loud.

'One of our girls was raped last night — he tied her up — wore a mask. He had a knife.'

Jean shivered.

'What is the world coming to?'

Mercifully the Neller Wing she made for was well away from the crime scene.

Pam Mortimer's secretary smiled up at her and indicated a chair.

'I'll tell her you're here.'

Jean thumbed through one of the magazines until the door opened and Pam Mortimer stood there, dressed in a white blouse and dark slacks, her hair pulled back tightly, accentuating her widow's peak.

'Jean, good of you to come.'

Pam held the door open with her arm forcing Jean to pass her as she entered. It was only momentarily, but their bodies actually touched.

Jean walked quickly into the room with its bookcases, couch, desk and large plants.

Unlike James Larsson before her, she

didn't notice that there was no window, only an artificial one of glazed glass with lights behind it . . .

Pam called out to her receptionist.

'Can we have two coffees, please?'

She came in and closed the door behind her.

'Do sit down Jean — over here.'

She walked to the couch.

'It's much more comfortable.'

Reluctantly Jean followed, set her purse beside her.

'I thought James Larsson would be here?'

Pam sat in her chair, spun around to face her.

'He is, but I sent him off for a quick physiology test. He'll be back soon. I thought I'd wait until I'd found out from you how you're getting on with the search for accommodation?'

'Well, I haven't been able to get anywhere, I'm afraid, as I said last night on the phone.'

'Hmm.' Pam tapped her fingertips together.

Jean couldn't help noticing how long her nails were, and so beautifully contoured and varnished. Her own were cut short for work.

'I was hoping perhaps you'd have some out-of-hours contacts via patients — you've been in the city longer than I have.'

'Sorry, no.'

Jean found she had to look away from those intense blue eyes.

'In that case, I do hope you will be able to influence him, we need to be very careful with his treatment.'

'Me? Why should I be able to do that?'

Pam Mortimer found some sort of blemish on her trousered knee, scratched at it with one of the long fingernails.

'Well, he has a great feeling for you — not surprising really.'

Jean felt her cheeks colouring.

'What do you mean?'

There was a perfunctory tap on the door and the secretary came in with a small tray with two cups of coffee. When she withdrew Pam said,

'You were instrumental in his recovery.'

She lifted one of the mugs and held it out. Jean took the coffee. Pam Mortimer hesitated, then said. 'Forgive me for saying this — but I gather you're going through a difficult patch with your husband?'

Jean was taken aback.

'How did you know?'

Sensing her resentment Pam Mortimer pulled a face.

'Oops — sorry, I thought it was common knowledge.'

Jean looked down into the brown liquid as

if to find consolation.

'I suppose it is — you know what hospitals are like.'

'Indeed I do.' There was a degree of bitterness in Pam Mortimer's voice as she added,

'Anyway, if you need a shoulder to cry on, don't hesitate.'

Jean raised her mug and took a sip, mumbling, 'Thank you.'

The psychotherapist smiled.

'Good — now, about James Larsson. If we can't get anywhere for him to stay I want you to persuade him to remain here for a while — he'll listen to you.'

Frowning, Jean took another sip of coffee before replying.

'But surely, if he wants to go, can we stop him?'

Pam Mortimer pressed her lips together in a firm line.

'We can. He's ill — make no mistake about that. He needs a lot of professional help.'

'I see. Well, I'll do my best.'

'Good.'

Pam Mortimer swivelled in her chair and picked up a telephone, pressed for an extension.

'Melanie, find James Larsson and get him to come in here would you — tell him Doctor

Hacker is with me.'

She put the receiver down. There was a pause as she weighed up her words. Finally —

'Jean, we know nothing about him, his background — where he was born, brought up, what socio-economic group to put him in — is he married? And so on.'

Jean tilted her head to one side.

'Why not, you must have asked him?'

'Indeed we have. He just avoids giving a straight answer. Don't forget, he's been trained to be evasive, he knows all the verbal tricks of the trade.'

Jean suppressed what would have been a humourless giggle, but said,

'One professional against another, so to speak?'

Pam Mortimer gave a throaty chuckle.

'Touché. That's why, Jean, we need your help.'

'He trusts you. If you could build a rapport, find out about the real man behind the mask he's presenting to the world, it would help us to help him.'

Jean shook her head.

'How do you suggest I build this rapport?'

Pam Mortimer gestured with her free hand.

'I thought perhaps you might see him in your spare time — perhaps have a meal with him, take him for a drive, that sort of thing.

Apart from anything else, it will aid his recovery.'

Jean sat back.

'Good God, how will I do that without the man thinking I'm hitting on him?'

The words denied the surge of excitement in her blood.

'Leave that to me. Point is — would you do it?'

Jean was still thinking when the phone gave a buzz. Pam picked it up, listened, said, 'one moment.' She put her hand over the receiver —

'He's here. Well?'

Jean nodded. 'Yes . . . I'll do it.'

The psychotherapist smiled, took her hand away.

'Send him in.'

He stood before them, the corner of his mouth lifting up as he smiled and nodded.

'Ladies.'

Pam Mortimer got up, arm extended towards Jean.

'James, I think you know Doctor Hacker.'

'Yes.'

Pam moved to her desk, sat on the edge, and pointed to her vacated seat.

'Sit over there for a change.'

He did, eyes never leaving Jean.

Pam Mortimer said,

'Further to our previous little talk, James, about things in general, Doctor Hacker, as you know attended you during your initial admittance here. I'd like her to help us in your treatment. Would you mind?'

Would he mind? He'd smelt the roses as he'd entered the room. It was all going like he'd expected, knew that The Devil herself would finally make her play.

He had a secret chuckle. Not many knew that: the devil — a *female*.

Larsson nodded.

'Anything you suggest, Pam.'

Jean found to her amazement that hearing him call the psychotherapist by her first name sparked a surge of jealousy.

'Good.'

Pam Mortimer picked up his file, began thumbing through the pages.

Jean was taken aback by the speed at which they'd arrived at this point.

In the quiet she flicked a nervous glance at Larsson, saying,

'I've got a confession to make. I've not been able to find you accommodation at the moment, would you mind staying here for just another night?'

He didn't immediately reply. Suddenly Jean was aware that his hands were shaking slightly as he said,

'I need to get out into the open air — the real country, with earth beneath my feet, and fresh air. Indoors I feel trapped.'

Pam Mortimer snapped the file shut.

'Of course. Perhaps you'd like to go for a walk — today, if Doctor Hacker can oblige. She knows all the good places to go around here.'

Amazed, Jean swung round to face her.

'Pam, I've got to work — it's my anesthetics day.'

She turned back to him again, adding lamely,

'I'm afraid I don't finish until five o'clock.'

Brightly Pam said,

'Early evening, that would be fine, wouldn't it James?'

Larsson looked anxiously at her.

'If it's not too much trouble?'

There was a pause, then she heard herself say,

'Not at all.'

Flustered Jean looked at her watch, stood up.

'I've got to go.'

On impulse, she stuck her hand out.

'Till later then.'

He took her hand, and they shook, just once as she said,

'I'll come around to reception, here, at

about 5.30. Is that all right?'

His eyes never left hers as he said, 'I look forward to it.'

Jean flushed. Both were aware that he held her hand for fractionally longer than was necessary.

10

Charles Seigle looked up from the male cadaver he was disembowelling with practised efficiency, dissecting the areas he wanted so he could display a section of the colon to the gallery.

All the time as he went through his running commentary, he scanned the faces in the rows above him. Was one of them the peeping tom?

The two girls were there, Mary and Annabel, taking copious notes as female students often did. He had unfinished business with them as well.

Finally he threw down his scalpel and stepped back.

'There you have it. That's all for today.'

As he moved away to his washbasin he flicked his head to the girls, motioning them to come round to his office door. They glanced uneasily at each other as everybody stood up, and the technicians moved in on the body, one hosing it down as the other got ready with needle and coarse black thread clamped in forceps.

In his room Seigle swept some books aside

on his desk, pushed his chair back, and put his feet up. There was a knock on the door.

'Come.'

The girls entered, looking strained.

'Close the door.'

As the blonde advanced towards him, the brunette turned, looking anxiously at the corridor before complying.

'What do you want?'

'Have you heard anything? Anybody say anything — look oddly at you?'

The girls shook their heads in unison.

'No,' said the blonde, 'but we've been talking it over. We're not going to get involved again — there's too much risk.'

Seigle grunted. Despite his fears he wanted more of these two.

'Come here tonight — late, say nine o'clock.'

He ran his tongue suggestively over his teeth.

'And make sure you wear something pretty underneath.'

He dropped his legs to the floor as he saw that they were wavering, and leaned forward onto his elbows. His voice took on heavy emphasis.

'That's if you want to get on, and do well here, and I can influence some of my colleagues as well.'

There could be no doubting the inference.

The brunette suddenly shot a defiant glance at her friend.

'All right. I'll come.'

With that she made for the door, flung it open. She turned back to the blonde who was still in front of the desk staring at Seigle.

'Coming?'

The blonde tossed her head, and without a word spun around and followed the brunette.

Seigle eyed her tight little butt until she turned to close the door.

'Something pretty,' he called.

The door slammed.

Slowly his face lost its smile, turned sour.

The office became silent, penetrated only by the noises of the clearing-up going on outside. It always reminded him of a dairy being cleaned, the sound of hosed water and brushes on concrete, the clatter of the trolleys like that of the metal crates they'd used when he'd had a vacation job on a farm as a student.

His thoughts turned to Jean Hacker. He knew that Steven had left her. He grunted. It had come as no surprise to him as it had to many. He had wondered about Steven Hacker for some time.

Seigle knew with a sureness of all his previous experiences what, deep down, the feisty Jean Hacker wanted, what that wet of a husband could never give her.

A strong man.

A *forceful* man.

⋆   ⋆   ⋆

Dr Steven Hacker looked down at his notes, then up to the students sitting in a semi-circle around him. Behind was the screen, which still carried the last slide of a stained section of a parotid gland.

He nodded and the technician turned off the projector.

'That about wraps it up for this morning.'

There was much closing of books and standing up, and he had to raise his voice to add,

'Don't forget, we're having a viva on Friday — anything from the past month including the fifth and seventh cranial nerves and associated tissues.'

He checked his watch. Since he'd left Jean he'd avoided the cafeteria or anywhere they might have a chance encounter.

But the person he was meeting, in response to an urgent call, would be at their secret place by now.

He didn't have much time to spare.

Jean entered the surgical changing-room and made for her green locker. She took off her bits of jewellery first, putting her rings and bracelets into a small box on the top shelf alongside her purse.

She changed slowly, slipping out of her skirt and blouse. It was as she was tying her hair back that she suddenly became aware of a feeling of not being alone, that she was being watched.

She looked around. Only rows of lockers confronted her. Rattled, she walked to the end of the middle row and peered around.

Empty.

Jean stomped angrily to the pile of green surgical scrubs on a shelf, and took a set.

What on earth was the matter with her?

But as she pushed her feet into white theatre boots she knew what it was that was disturbing her.

Her appointment that evening.

A walk with James Larsson. She felt excitement and apprehension.

A walk on the wild side.

A walk into the unknown.

★ ★ ★

When she left the changing-room it fell silent. But there was movement behind the grille high in the wall.

And a flash of reflected light —

On metal.

*　*　*

In the anesthetic bay Jean met her first patient being wheeled in by the orderlies. As she greeted the woman her fingers were automatically reaching for the patient's wrist, checking her pulse.

The patient smiled in a distant dreamy sort of way, already feeling the effects of her pre-med. Satisfied with the pulse, Jean wrapped a tourniquet of yellow velcro tape around the woman's right upper arm, and started to examine the back of her hand, first stroking it speculatively, and then slapping it gently until the engorged veins were clearly visible. Jean held her own hand out.

'Right nurse, give me a point eight infusion set.'

With the patient safely intubated, Jean was adjusting the flow meters controlling the relative supply of oxygen and nitrous oxide when a muffled voice boomed out behind her,

'Jean, are you all right?'

She turned.

The figure was dressed like all of them, but was bigger. Simon Limbach was easily recognizable even though only his eyes, in the narrow slit of skin between cap and mask, were visible; they seemed enlarged by his glasses. He regarded her steadily as she answered.

'Yes, why what's the matter?'

He started checking the trays of instruments the scrub nurse was setting out.

'This dreadful rape, it's scared a lot of the staff.'

The *rape*. Jean had forgotten about it.

Simon Limbach reached for a scalpel, and examined the blade, its handle lost in his large hand.

It glinted as a nurse manoeuvred the brilliant overhead lights onto the rectangle of skin bordered by the green linen she had draped over the patient's belly, the site, despite being painted with antiseptic, dazzling in the pool of focused beams.

His eyes found hers.

'Marjorie — my secretary — hasn't come in today and she isn't answering her phone. If anything has happened to her . . . '

With a swiftness that startled Jean, he turned to the patient, and drew the blade across the offered skin in a wide sweep.

For a split-second the thin red line stayed the same, then widened like an opening mouth.

★   ★   ★

James Larsson lay on his bed, hands at his sides, staring up at the ceiling.

Unseeing.

His eyes were wide, fixed, the pupils black holes. The dream state had returned like a ripple over his consciousness, a ripple of vivid clarity, everything brighter, louder, more painful than before. And as always, a high-pitched tinkling like some fluttering Chinese mobile in a breeze.

Only it was his nerves playing the tune. Nightmare images fused with reality and became his reality.

He was tied spread-eagled on a table, dark sweating faces looming over him. The pain came again.

Larsson's body arched up, mouth open in a silent scream as the electric current coursed through his body.

Again,

And again,

And again.

He had sought death, he knew what he was doing when he had returned to the valley.

Death was the only way to release himself from the agony of his loss, and to be with his dear wife once more.

But then had come the pain they had inflicted on him, pain, and the mysterious woman from Al Qaeda dressed in her all-concealing black burka, who directed them.

All-concealing, except her hands. That was what had been so extraordinary. They were *white*.

And her scent, that was of roses.

As his torture continued, something inside him made him determined not to let them win.

Not to let *her* win.

And if he could — to kill her.

★ ★ ★

The rescue force came in the early hours of the morning. They had hidden in the rock-strewn hillside all through the day, observing the comings and goings through special binoculars that never reflected the burning sun.

The night before they had parachuted into the next valley, using a high altitude, high opening technique involving breathing apparatus that meant there had been no aircraft noise to spook the enemy. Using night vision goggles they had trekked in the moonless dark before taking up their positions over-looking the village.

When they struck it was with terrifying, ruthless efficiency, one group making directly for the compound where the Taliban fighters lay sleeping, the others, straight for the stone building where they knew Larsson was held prisoner.

They threw stun grenades through the open windows, which gave a flash of intense, brilliant light as they detonated with a stupefying crack.

The guards, blinded and disorientated, were swiftly cut down with bullets and knives.

The captain leading the raid reached Larsson, took one look and yelled, 'Medic'.

In truth, he thought they were too late. By the time the three recovery helios thundered in at dawn and they scrambled aboard, eighteen Taliban fighters were dead.

Only the women's quarters had been spared.

Larsson knew *she* had not been there when they had burst in.

Though her face had always been covered, he would know her again.

By the scent of roses.

Larsson swallowed.

Exactly the same as Dr Jean Hacker.

Jean.

He frowned. How was it possible? How had she got here?

But there could be no doubt.

And there had been a final heart-stopping shock — with her face at last free of the veil there was something about her that reminded him of his dead wife.

His *beloved* wife.

Tears came into his eyes. Why had God done this, cruelly twisting the knife that had already pierced his heart?

Death still remained the only solution.

And he would take her with him.

But the thought, instead of making him feel good, somehow unsettled him. He broke out into a sweat, the sun coming through the windows in his room seeming to burn fiercer — like the sun in Afghanistan — except there was no window in his room.

He began to sob. Perhaps he was dead already — and in hell, doomed to exist in perpetual torment?

Larsson struggled to get himself under control. It took time, but in the end he sat up, swung his legs around, sat head bowed for a moment.

Slowly he got his feet to the floor, testing his weight on them. Strength flowed in his muscles.

He made for the bathroom. It was only then that he realized his hand still gripped something.

He looked down, puzzled.

It was the screwdriver.

11

Jean pulled off her paper hat and binned it, undid the tape at her waist and unwound the smock. She threw it into the used basket and made for the basins.

Two women were busy cleaning their hands, shaking off excess water and elbowing their taps shut as she reached them.

Jean knew them both and nodded. The nearest woman in her late-fifties, in a green T-shirt and pyjama-type surgery trousers, was a Gynae consultant, in whose department Jean took a turn in the Well Woman Clinic.

'We were just talking about the terrible attack on one of our nurses. Poor little girl was lucky to escape with her life.'

Her companion grunted.

'When they catch him I'd dearly like to have him on my table. He wouldn't be able to torment another defenceless young woman.'

It carried all the more weight since she was one of the State's leading uro-genital surgeons.

Jean suddenly felt clammy.

'Phew is it me, or is it just getting stuffy in here?'

The gynaecologist nodded her agreement. 'Now that you mention it, it is a bit hot.' She looked up at the grille in the wall.

'The bloody ventilation is on the blink again. Have to get the maintenance people to have another look.'

She grumbled on.

'This place was built on the cheap.'

She crossed the room, stood on a bench seat and raised a hand, waving it in front of the grille.

'Not a bit of air coming through here — it might as well be blocked.'

* * *

Jean had taken care with her appearance — realizing as she did so the implication.

She got in the car, drove slowly around the perimeter road till she reached the separate parking lot for the Neller Wing. With a last, discreet, check in the mirror she got out and made for the entrance, seeing her reflection in its smoked glass doors, unaware that she was being observed.

From a window above, Pam Mortimer looked down on Jean Hacker as she neared the building.

As did James Larsson from his position in the hall.

Jean pushed through, didn't see him for a second until he moved clear of the large palm-type tree.

'So you came?'

She cocked her head to one side.

'Why — didn't you think I would?'

He looked tired, drawn, worse than in the morning, and evaded the question by asking another.

'Do I need boots? I've only got these trainers.'

He pointed down then indicated the sweater, blue jeans and an ex-army combat jacket.

'Friends of the Hospital.'

She chuckled.

'You look fine — better than the stuff you came in, so I believe.'

He grunted.

'No doubt anything would be better than what I came in.'

She only nodded her agreement, aware of the physical attraction she felt and knew it was stupid.

She was a mature, professional woman.

But she was divorcing, therefore vulnerable.

Jean Hacker smiled at the receptionist.

'I'll have him back by seven.'

James Larsson held the heavy door open

with one hand — effortlessly.

'Sounds like I'm being taken out of school by my favourite aunt.'

Jean winced.

As she led the way to the car, outwardly the purposeful doctor carrying out her promise, Jean's legs felt weak. They didn't improve much in the car, her knees, peeping out below her hemline, to her humiliation were trembling. She prayed that he couldn't see them. But if truth were told, she'd thought of nothing else all day but this moment.

He got into the passenger seat, making her conscious of the cramped interior.

As they did the seat belts up their hands touched.

Jean started the engine, put it into drive and moved off as he asked,

'Is it a long way?'

'Normally take twenty minutes — but it's the rush hour.'

She tuned in the radio. Soft, slow music filtered into the car, helping to fill the silence and covering the sound of her heart, pounding away in her chest like the over-reactive pump it was.

As Jean concentrated on the heavy traffic, he seemed to be staring out at the empty litter-filled side streets that were the city's tough area.

When they finally turned up her road the

evening sun was flicking through the passing trees, almost like a strobe light.

She remembered her training and hearing tales of touring cars in the 1930s crashing for no apparent reason on the straight roads of France, and how it had finally been put down to the strong sunlight flickering through the rows of tall poplars, triggering epileptic attacks in the drivers.

She glanced at him, but Larsson seemed normal — unaffected.

'Here we are.'

With practised efficiency she swept into the drive.

The shock of seeing Steven's car at the front door was like a physical blow in the pit of her stomach. She pushed the auto into park and switched off the engine.

'Will you excuse me for a moment? I won't be long.'

She got out, ran in through the half-open front door.

'Steven.'

She went to the bottom of the stairs.

'Steven — is that you?'

There was no reply.

'Steven.'

She went into the drawing-room.

It was tidy, untouched.

'Steven — where are you?'

Through the open double doors she could see into the dining-room. The empty chairs and bare, polished table looked back at her.

Jean stuck her head into the kitchen; saw through the big windows out up the lawn to the wood as she tried again.

'Hello — Steven?'

The strange emptiness was overpowering. She moved back into the hall, the grandfather clock's steady measure the only noise in the absolute quiet. She began to ascend the stairs, reached the top.

'Steven.'

Her voice faltered. He must be in his own room since she could see into the master bedroom. Jean reached out, put her hand on the knob, and walked in.

'Steven . . . '

It was empty.

Jean went to the window, looked out, down at her car and James Larsson, elbow just visible, and there, beside it, was Steven's BMW. So she wasn't dreaming.

She swung round — straight into the figure of a man right behind her.

She gave out a piercing scream.

Steven Hacker held her wildly flailing arms by the wrists.

'What's the matter Jean — jumpy, aren't you?'

She snatched herself free, rubbing at the soreness where his iron grip had caught her.

'Where the hell were you?'

He moved to the window, pulled the curtain back a fraction and looked down at the drive.

'In the loft — there were some things I needed.'

Jean got control of herself.

'What things — and I thought you had left?'

'Books — and a few items of sentimental value.'

He turned back, jerked his head at the window and murmured.

'Well, you haven't wasted any time have you?'

She snapped.

'He's a patient.'

He chuckled.

She felt she had to explain.

'He's in Neller Wing. Pam Mortimer asked me to help — give him some fresh air away from the hospital.'

Steven raised one eyebrow in that annoying habit of his, said sarcastically —

'Pam Mortimer? Since when have you two been *friendly*?'

The implication cut into her like a knife.

Jean turned on her heel and went down the

stairs, called over her shoulder,

'You bastard. I hope you will have the decency to call me before you come for anything else.'

He came to the landing banisters, leaned on his elbows and shouted down,

'I've got everything now.'

She went through to the kitchen, came back with a pair of low-heeled walking shoes.

'Good, because I'm changing the locks.'

She stormed out, slamming the front door behind her.

Steven Hacker moved back to the bedroom window, watched as she opened her driver's door, and sat on the seat, legs outside, changing her shoes, talking all the time to the man in the passenger seat whose face he couldn't see.

When she finally stood up and closed her door, the man got out. He was of average height, well built, but not bulky. The man turned slowly and like a robot raised his face to the window.

Hacker stepped away, let the curtain fall back into place.

There was something in the man's eyes that unnerved him.

12

Jean led the way along the path as it wound its way deeper into the wood.

For a minute the silence between them was broken only by the sound of the unseen birds high in the tops of the trees, and the snap of the occasional twig under Jean's foot, yet she felt at ease, comfortable.

She led the way making for a stream and its small waterfall a mile ahead, up under the steeply rising hill, where it turned into limestone cliffs.

'How large is this forest?'

His voice brought her back from angry thoughts of Steven. Jean brushed aside an overhanging branch.

'Pretty big. Goes as far as the State line twenty miles away.'

'You're lucky to live right at the edge.'

She shrugged.

'My husband and I are splitting up, so we shall have to sell. In any case, I'm not sure I would walk in here on my own — so close to the city — you hear of such terrible things these days.'

He wondered, was this the right moment to kill her?

It would be so easy.

And they would never find her, he would see to that.

He frowned, puzzled. Something was holding him back.

The path meandered through great oaks and elms, with ferns crowding in on all sides, and toadstools glinting like mines in the dark earth.

After a quarter of a mile the track twisted sharply around an outcrop of rock, and began to climb more steeply.

He watched her as she leaned into the hillside, catching a tuft of grass with one hand to help her up the gradient. Her slim straight back and neat body was so like his wife's.

He swallowed, turned his eyes away . . . and caught sight of something moving through the trees far to the left, parallel to their path.

A dark figure moving with stealth, across a small clearing full of flowers.

Were they shadowing him — waiting to see what he would do?

He did nothing, said nothing, and kept going, until Jean suddenly slipped back into him.

He steadied her with his hands on her waist, his face close to her hair.

Jean recovered quickly, bent lower and

using both hands on the grass scrambled forward.

It was the first time that his hands had touched her body. He'd smelt the roses again, and this time the freshness of that cloud of auburn hair.

She reached the top of the bank.

'Shall we stop here awhile, I'm not as fit as I should be?'

Larsson nodded, could see no sign of the figure. He scanned above them, where the ascending trees changed to conifers, tightly packed, intensely dark, where nothing grew on the floor and only pine needles formed a deep carpet.

'Come and sit down.'

He lowered himself beside her, facing the sun as it sank behind the blue hills on the horizon.

She reclined back on her elbows, one leg raised, bent at the knee, and a piece of grass between her lips.

It was a good time, she realized, to find out more about him — not just for his treatment, but because she wanted to know for herself.

'Where do you come from James?'

He was running his hand over a rock lying between them.

'Oh, all over — my father was in the military.'

With that he rolled the rock aside and picked at something that was moving away from the light.

Without thinking, he lifted the small wriggling creature to his mouth — and ate it.

It was only then that he saw her horrified face.

He scratched at his chin, gestured in embarrassment.

'Sorry. Old habits die hard.'

Jean swallowed.

'Habits?'

'Well — training. There is lots here to eat if you know what you are looking for.'

She shuddered, brought her other leg up and sat forward, arms wrapped around her knees.

She was curled up with that flexible ease that women seemed to have, and was so pleasurable to observe. And despite what he knew, and what he would have to do, this woman was magnificent.

Suddenly she said, 'I love the summer.'

He smiled self-consciously.

'Summer is a woman, winter the man. They complement each other.'

She giggled. 'How poetic of you.'

Jean lay back again, arms at her side, stared up at the passing clouds. It was some time before his head appeared.

It had come sooner than she had expected, but . . .

Would he . . . ?

Then he came closer, and their lips touched. Her eyelids fluttered, closed. It lasted only a few seconds, before he drew away, stayed above her as her eyes re-opened. They stared at each other.

Nothing was said. Nothing needed to be said. Finally he rolled away and lay back onto his elbows.

James Larsson was confused. He knew she was the enemy but there *was* something between them. When it came to it, could he kill her?

She chuckled.

'I've never been kissed by a patient before.'

'Well, you have now.'

Jean turned onto her side to see him. Again nature made its presence felt.

He could not but help noticing the steep curve of her hip, plunging down into the valley of her waist and up again to her small breasts. And as ever the rich crown of reddish hair fell around her pale neck.

'And you went into the army too, like your father?'

He nodded, eyes dropping to the lips he'd just touched with his own as they moved again.

'Did you go to West Point?'

He chuckled,

'What's so funny?'

'I went in as an enlisted man, as a private. I got my commission later.'

Even Jean realized that that must have been a tough route. She did not know enough about military matters, even if he had told her, to realize just how extraordinary it was that James Larsson should now be a major.

But then, battlefield commissions were, out of declared wartime, very rare. James Larsson's walk on the wild side had been in Iraq.

He suddenly got to his feet and scanned around. His action disappointed Jean, broke the closeness.

He held out his hand for her. She took it, and found herself gently, effortlessly, hauled to her feet.

'Come on, let's go higher.'

He did not immediately release his grip on her hand.

She was pleased about that.

And something seemed to have happened to him. Whereas before he had dragged along behind her, he now led.

It was as if he had turned a corner and was getting better. Jean felt a weight coming off her own shoulders, lightening her step.

They reached the cliff face with a small stream coming down the rocks to end in a pool the size of a tennis court.

Jean moved nearer the spraying cascade, called over her shoulder,

'There are some caves around here.'

He stayed where he was.

In the mud at the edge of the pool was a footprint.

A *new* footprint.

Slowly filling with water.

13

He looked around; he saw nothing but trees, rock, sky.

And her.

Jean reached a boulder, climbed on it and stretched out her arms, fingers in the falling water.

Larsson came over to her, watched as she played her hands in the glittering torrent.

'Well, Doctor, what about you?'

Still with her hands cupping and uncupping in the spray she said,

'You mean my life?'

He nodded.

She jutted out her lower lip.

'Nothing much really. Passed all my exams like a good girl, met my husband to be, qualified, married — you know the rest.'

Indeed he did, but he hadn't expected her to reveal her darker side — how she had been drawn to radical Islam. He would find that out later.

'What about kids?'

She shook her head.

'No, Steven always said we couldn't afford them and in any case . . . '

Her voice tapered off. There was no way she could bring herself to say that their sex life had been . . . less than satisfactory.

She brought her hands in from the cold water and pressed them to her forehead, then her cheeks.

'And you — did you have children before . . .'

Jean couldn't finish it but he did. The bitterness in his voice was like acid

' . . . before my wife died? No. We planned . . . were . . . about to start.'

The tears ran down his cheeks.

She reached out to comfort him, held him as his body silently convulsed.

He was conscious of her slim figure, the first time he had been in an embrace with a woman since . . . the cruel irony did not escape him.

They were like that as the first whisper of moving scree came. Jean would have run out — into the path of the large rocks that crashed down with a roar like an express train. Instead, he pinned her into the cliff face, covered her with his body as the rocks thundered down.

As soon as it was finished he snapped.

'Stay put,' and leapt away, running and turning, searching the escarpment.

Nothing. It was empty.

Jean took a gulp of air, shook the dust from her hair. Despite his order she followed him.

'My God, that was extraordinary.'

She looked as if she was going to faint, so he put his arm protectively around her shoulder and decided not to say anything about the figure, and the footprint.

★ ★ ★

Back at the house Jean was relieved to see that Steven's car had gone. They crunched across the gravel drive.

She got her keys out.

'You'll come in, won't you? How about a nice cup of tea?'

While she busied herself he wandered to the window, looked out at the garden.

'You're very secluded here.'

She fetched down cups from the hooks on an old Welsh dresser, and placed them on saucers.

'Yes, I shall miss that.'

He turned as she got a milk carton from the fridge and filled a small jug.

'Where will you go?'

She shrugged. 'We'll have to see. In any case it will take some time to sell this place.'

The kettle boiled. Jean hung three tea bags in the pot and poured in the water. With everything assembled she carried the tray to the pine table, set it down, and pulled out a chair. Larsson sat opposite.

'Would you like a cookie?'

Jean reached for a tin on the end of the counter and opened it, offering it to Larsson.

He took one and then watched as she poured.

They talked and drank tea. It was all so normal, so peaceful. She was so different from the woman who had tormented him to the point of madness.

What was her game? What was it she wanted? Well, he would wait.

Finally, Jean went upstairs to tidy her face. Larsson wandered into the family room, then the dining-room and looked down the garden. He checked the lock on the french windows, then the windows themselves. They would be no problem when the time came.

Jean used the en-suite bathroom then went to her dressing-table, dashed a bit more colour onto her lips, gave her hair a violent brushing, thought about tying it back, changed her mind and left, turning the light off.

The windowless en-suite bathroom was plunged into total darkness.

The figure standing in the shower with the curtain pulled did not move, even when the front door had closed and the sound of the car engine, and the tyres on the gravel had long faded. The figure remained as the house fell silent as the grave.

★ ★ ★

It was slate blue dusk as she drew up outside the entrance to Neller Wing. Lights shone all over the hospital complex.

Jean looked around, but could see no one she knew. Since they had last been here several hours ago so much had changed between them.

As he got out, Jean said hesitantly —

'I'll see you tomorrow then?'

He leaned down, one arm on the roof.

'If you don't — I'll have a relapse.'

Relieved, she became sheepish.

'We can't have that. What would you like to do?'

His eyes seemed to drop to her legs resting on the pedals, making her wonder what was coming, then he said — 'How about a good meal — I haven't sat in a restaurant for a very long time?'

Jean was delighted. It was something she also hadn't done herself for longer than she cared to remember.

'That would be fun. We'll have to make it

early, about 6, and if Doctor — Pam — agrees. I've got the afternoon free, so I could pick you up at, say, one o'clock.'

He nodded, just the once and smiled.

'OK. Goodnight Jean.'

'Goodnight, James.'

He stood up, and shut the door.

Jean put the gear stick into drive and moved off. In the rear mirror she saw that he just stood there, watching. He was unmoving even as she turned the corner of the buildings.

That made her feel good.

* * *

At the top of the hill her headlights picked up the start of the trail which she and James had walked earlier.

As she turned the steering wheel, the beams raked down the wild hedgerow at the front of the house, and then into the drive. She drove straight into the garage, its walls closing around her.

Jean cut the engine and the lights, plunging the interior of the garage into blackness.

When she opened the driver's door the courtesy light lit up the interior. She got out, slammed it shut, putting herself back into darkness. Using the remote she locked the door, the red lights flashing twice. Jean edged past the car and out into the drive. It was a pitch black night, the stars obscured by cloud. Only after she got the front door open, and reached the switch, did light flood out.

She threw her keys into the bowl on the hall table and pushed on into the kitchen. When the fluorescent tube stopped flickering her eyes fell onto the table, their cups and the now cold teapot. She paused, holding his cup for a second — wondering. Would anything really come of it?

She made a mug of instant coffee and took it upstairs with her.

In the bedroom she quickly undressed and wandered naked with her drink into the en-suite bathroom, taking a sip of it and setting it down on the vanity unit.

Jean's mind was on James Larsson and the future as she made for the shower and tore back the curtain.

The figure lunged downwards and reached her before she realized what was happening, but by then it was too late.

Arms wrapped around her as she fell back screaming, the loathsome, grinning face pressed against her own in an obscene kiss.

She rolled free from its embrace, got up, staggering backwards and wiping her mouth with the back of her hand.

A human skeleton.

She recognized it for what it was by the number stamped on its bony skull.

It was Steven's training specimen.

'Bastard.'

She screamed it out.

'Bastard.'

Her body shook, as she stood racked by sobs.

Then with a defiant last, 'Bastard' she picked up the skeleton and carried it to his room, flung it down on his bed, and stormed back to the bathroom.

What an idiotic fool he'd made of her. First thing in the morning she'd have the locks changed. She couldn't be putting up with his nonsense — not knowing whether he was going to be there or not.

Naked and feeling cold she stepped in the cubicle, pulled the plastic curtain across and turned on the water.

Facing the wall mounted jet, Jean let the hot spray fall onto her breasts and run down over her belly.

Eyes closed she turned slowly around, revelling in the exhilarating sting as it coursed down her back and ran in flooding rivulets between the cheeks of her bottom.

She opened her eyes. The steam was solid, condensing on the plastic curtain.

Despite the heat, Jean suddenly felt icy. In her mind she saw that frightening blurred figure in the film *Psycho* — knife raised as it came at the woman in the shower, and the blood clouding the water as it whirled around and drained away.

She snatched the curtain open.

The room was empty.

14

James Larsson had watched the tail-lights of her car until they had disappeared from sight. Then he had turned and stood looking at the entrance to Neller Wing. They would be waiting to check him back in and would know if he didn't appear.

He looked to the trees and bushes of the grounds. They had served their purpose, but his heart now lay in the real forest and hills to the west — and the woman who lived at their foot. Larsson strode in, the security guard stood with his arms behind his back in front of the counter.

'Been waiting for you.'

'Why — what's up?'

The man looked at his watch.

'You were supposed to be in half an hour ago.'

He shrugged.

'You'll have to speak to my doctor — I was with her.'

The man grunted, said no more as Larsson bade him goodnight and walked down the corridor.

He was aware of being watched as he

entered his room. No sooner was he inside with the door shut, than there was a click: The electronic lock had been activated.

Smiling, Larsson stripped for bed, conscious that there was a camera trained on him. When he'd finished his ablutions he turned out the light, got in under the covers and waited.

An hour passed before he stepped silently out and found the screwdriver in his pants.

He'd taken it from a workman's open toolbox he'd found by an open ventilation grille.

By touch only, he began to undo the screws he had already loosened the night before.

When he'd removed the plate he levered the bolt back, and jammed it open with a dime.

He began to dress.

★ ★ ★

Jean was fast asleep, lying on her side, face caught in the soft glow of the bedside alarm clock.

Outside the room, the landing and the top of the stairs were dark, silent, only the faintest of light entering from the now starlit windows, revealing mysterious lumps and shapes that in daytime were familiar objects — a chair, a sidetable, a vase.

At the bottom of the stairs there was utter

blackness and, in the intervals between the slow deep beats of the grandfather clock — absolute silence.

In the family room, down behind a sofa, a movement came, a tiny point of quivering flesh that projected from a gap between floor and skirting boards: a nose.

It smelt no danger.

More of the mouse appeared, first whiskers, then beady eyes darting from side to side, ears straining for any minute sound.

There was none, even when the handle on the French windows began to turn down slowly. It reached the bottom of its run, held unmoving, then —

The shrill noise was like a scalpel slicing through the night air, freezing everything it came into contact with — the trembling nose of the mouse, the breathing of Jean Hacker — and the handle.

The telephone.

Jean shot up — for a moment totally confused.

Downstairs the door handle jumped back. There was no sign of the mouse.

Turning on the bedside light she reached for the receiver, nearly dropping it before she finally got it to her ear.

'Hello.'

'Doctor Jean Hacker?'

It was a man's voice.

'Yes.'

'This is the hospital. We've just gone into condition red. All Emergency Room staff are being asked to report immediately.'

Jean managed to clear her mind.

'What's happened?'

'There's been a derailment of a sleeper train. We've been notified by ambulance control that casualties are moderate to heavy. The hospital is on take.'

'Right, I'm on my way.'

Jean dressed quickly and went downstairs. In the hall cupboard she found a coat, then picked up her car keys from the bowl. She switched on the porch light, and flung open the front door.

Outside it was cool, the clouds had now gone to reveal a sky full of stars. She scurried along the side of the house, shoes crunching on the gravel until she reached the open garage doors. In seconds the engine burst into life and she reversed out.

The red tail-lights of her car disappeared down the hill, leaving only the porch light to break the darkness, revealing the trees looming out of the mist, looking like ghostly, mist-shrouded sentinels.

And something else.

A shadowy figure.

Madness.

Jean joined the other bleary-eyed, white-faced members of the Emergency Room teams as they assembled in their pre-arranged area. The place was otherwise deserted, apart from a drunk.

Phones, unanswered, were ringing all over the place.

The ramps by the ambulance reception area remained empty.

Simon Limbach arrived, looking surprisingly fresh. A nurse groaned to the others out of earshot.

'Holy Joe looks good day or night — what's his secret?'

He came over to Jean.

'My dear, pulled you from your warm bed, eh?'

She winced. He had managed to make warm bed sound suggestive.

Outside a blue light suddenly flickered, the ambulance sweeping in, and then reversing back to the ramp. A second blue light flashed, then two more. Jean felt sick with expectancy as they moved forward, waiting for the vehicles to open their doors.

Like an army about to clash, she thought. It was the last abstract idea she had that night.

And then they came, a never ending tide of

broken, bleeding humanity that threatened at one time to engulf them. There had been four hundred and fifty people on the train, and a very high proportion had suffered the effects of the violent braking; many others were more seriously injured in the one coach that had been crushed. It was to be another hour before any of them were cut free from the wreckage.

She was released from duty at dawn when another hospital took over the reception of the remaining casualties.

Jean sat with a cup of coffee in the staff room as they all unwound, some stretched back in the leather chairs or curled up on the floor.

She set her cup down on the table beside her chair and stood up.

'Right, I'm going home to freshen-up.'

The women she had been talking with glanced at each other.

'Is Steven all right?'

She knew it was coming of course. Word was well around by now.

'As far as I'm aware, yes. I don't know where he's living — but he was back last night collecting stuff.'

They made noises of sympathy. Jean thanked them, and grabbed her coat.

It was lighter as she drove home, and

according to the radio it looked as though it was going to be hot with a warm front moving in. Jean ached from bending over, debriding wounds, suturing, setting up drips. There was one thing she wanted more than anything else — a hot bath.

The porch light was now only a pale globe in the half-light.

She threw her keys into the hall bowl, ran up the stairs, checked the time again. She had an hour and a half before her shift started.

Jean spun the taps and stuck in the plug. The water was flowing in, steam rising as she took off her clothes and collecting them up, threw them into the laundry basket. She pulled on a towelling robe and thought — drink.

She ran lightly downstairs and entered the family room. The French door handle was just beside her as she fixed a gin and tonic. Back upstairs she set her drink down on the cork-topped seat, turned and removed the robe. She tested the water and found it too hot. While the cold tap roared out its stronger jet she sprinkled bath salts into the water and swirled it with her hand.

On impulse she went naked to fetch her nail file from the dressing-table. She never bothered to draw the drapes at the back.

A blackbird bounced jauntily across the

lawn, stopping frequently, head on one side as if listening, beady eye continually on the lookout for danger.

It was near the edge of the forest that it struck, stabbing its beak into the ground, closing over the exposed end of a fat worm.

The struggle began, but it was one sided. Inch by inch the worm was pulled clear — until Jean, naked, paused by her dressing-table.

Suddenly the copse right by the blackbird moved, a grunt betraying the presence of something the alert bird had not detected.

Screeching, it flew away in panic.

The green and brown combat jacket blended perfectly with the shrubbery. The white face that might have alerted the bird to its danger was covered by a camouflage mask used by snipers in jungle warfare, the wavy patches of green and brown rag broken by the almost comical straight nosepiece and the slits for the eyes.

Jean turned, and for one fleeting moment seemed to be staring straight down at the alien face, her pink-tipped breasts clearly in view.

Hissing, it shrank back. Then she swung away and disappeared.

Behind the slanting apertures the eyes glittered with a pitiless menace — like a snake.

Thankfully she eased her aching body into the welcoming embrace of the hot water and closed her eyes.

It had been a terrible night of suffering and carnage, with families rent by pain and death. The effects of exhaustion had begun its insidious growth in her mind.

Jean smiled as she dozed in the steam, sipping her drink. A few seconds ago, in the bedroom, as she leaned forward for her nail file, she'd glanced out of the window.

For one incredible moment she thought — would have sworn — she'd seen a bush move in the garden.

Actually move.

Jean giggled, knew it was the tension of the night coming out.

The news spread around the hospital like wildfire. During the main carnage, when everybody was working flat out, a man had undergone emergency surgery in the early hours of the morning for a deep stab wound which was quickly established as being made, not by a knife, but by some sort of pointed steel rod that had been thrust with great upward force into his abdomen.

He had staggered into ER leaving a thick trail of blood that security traced back to a window that had been forced open in the nurses' quarters.

The man was rambling on about a man who had come out of the dark, put an arm around his neck and pulled him up onto his toes before the 'knife' had gone in.

Was his attacker some sort of vigilante, or an accomplice he had fallen out with?

But one thing was for sure, the assault had been ferocious, and professional, and there was a general feeling that another rape had been prevented.

The relief among the female staff was palpable — and short lived.

15

'Did you enjoy your evening with Dr Hacker?'

James Larsson sat erect.

'Very much so. It was good to get out into the country again.'

Pam Mortimer nodded, then carried on reading her notes. He waited. A lot of patients would have become restless.

Not him.

He sat there, hands on knees, unmoving.

She picked up the brown envelope with the Government logo that she had received that morning, and slipped out the letter and the photograph.

The letter was from the Army giving Larsson's details, as much as was commensurate with security.

But it was enough.

Pam Mortimer looked up.

'Let's see, you were in Iraq before the deployment to Afghanistan, is that correct?'

'Yes.'

He didn't enquire of her about the letter she was so obviously holding. Others would have. He just sat there, waiting.

Pam Mortimer decided on a direct approach. This man was, after all, trained to contain himself, to control not only his own reactions, but if possible, those around him.

'It's a long list of valiant service to your country.'

'Thank you.'

'You must enjoy your work?'

He didn't say anything.

'You like . . . killing?'

'No.'

'Come now, you are in the army.'

Larsson's mouth drew up in a sardonic smile.

She continued to leaf through the notes.

'I believe that people like yourself — *specialists* — is that right?'

He corrected her.

'Special Forces.'

'Yes, well, that you deliberately create horrific injuries. For example I read somewhere that if you kill a terrorist you deliberately shoot him again, in the face so as to frighten others when they see the mutilated body.'

Larsson smiled.

'You don't want to believe everything you read.'

She frowned.

'But wouldn't you agree, that would be

terrible, inhuman, if it were true?'

He shrugged.

'Maybe. But have you ever seen the aftermath of what a bomb packed with nails can do in a shopping mall, or a subway? They need to be terrorized too.'

Pam Mortimer frowned.

'So you are saying you act like a terrorist?'

James Larsson did not reply.

Pam Mortimer, placed a photograph down in front of him.

'Do you think any of those young men would agree with you now?'

Larsson stared down at the four eager young men.

Four guys with fresh faces full of the promise and energy of youth, burning with life, confident in their unique skills reflected in the berets they wore with pride.

It had been taken in New Mexico after one of the earliest exercises in H.A.H.O. — high altitude, high opening parachuting, when as a 'stick' they had jumped at more than thirty thousand feet.

They had used oxygen and thermal suits to offset the extreme cold which would have killed them before they had drifted in a well calculated pattern some thirty miles, 'flying' their wing shaped parachutes in an exercise, an attack on a strong point held by Marines.

Just as they had done in his rescue.

They had taken the sentries completely by surprise. Albeit, they still had to make a fight of it with the Jarheads.

Afterwards, a glass or two in the base bar had settled things amicably.

Memories. Good friends, good comrades.

All gone — they were all gone.

Except him.

And he was a wreck — mentally.

'Well?'

Her voice snapped him back to the present.

'You'll have to ask them yourself.'

Quietly she said,

'But I can't, can I? They're all dead, and for what?'

Larsson looked steadily back at her.

Suddenly Pam Mortimer found herself shivering.

It was his eyes.

She changed the subject, tried to be brighter.

'Have you thought what you'd like to do today?'

At last Larsson shifted his weight in the chair.

'Have you not heard from Dr Hacker?'

Indeed she had. And that, if the truth were told, had unsettled her. Jean had called first thing.

Could she take him out for the afternoon — then they were going on to a restaurant for dinner?

It was the excitement in her voice that had rankled with Pam — excitement, and a certain warmth.

'Of course, Jean — *only* — ' She paused, allowing Jean to fill the interval.

'Only what?'

'I don't think I can allow him out for that. He's not really been assessed properly for ordinary community activity.'

Pam had sensed the disappointment in the hush before Jean had said,

'May I remind you it was at your suggestion I'm doing this, and I can tell you, away from the hospital he's even more normal.'

'I'm sorry Jean, but really, its too early, believe me.'

'Pam' — Jean's voice had been harsh. 'I *am* a doctor you know, not a member of the public. If I think there is in any way a sign that James is reacting to — '

'*James*'. The way she had used his first name stung Pam into cutting her off.

'Jean — psychology is *my* field, and I'm in charge of his therapy. There can be no discussion. I want him here tonight for another test at six o'clock sharp.'

She had added an appeal for sympathy.

'We're on a tight schedule. The army have asked me to give a report, and discharge him back to them as soon as possible.'

It was a lie.

Jean's answer had been flat, devoid of any warmth.

'Well, in that case I have no choice. I'll drop him back to the Wing on the dot of six.'

Pam Mortimer had known she had won — and lost. Desperate to try and salvage something she started to say,

'Thank you for understanding, Jean. Perhaps tomorrow we could all go — hello?'

The line was dead.

She came back to the present, watched him carefully as she answered.

'Yes. We agreed that the best action for today was another outing this afternoon. We decided that this evening would be — difficult.'

The lie came easily.

If she had expected a reaction she was to be disappointed.

Flatly, he said, 'I see.'

Pam Mortimer got up, automatically he followed suit. She came around to the door.

'I believe they want to do another blood and urine test as a follow-up. Could you go across to the laboratory please. Dr Hacker will be here at about one o'clock.'

He nodded as she opened the door saying over her shoulder as she went ahead,

'You heard all the commotion last night of course — that terrible train smash? It may mean Dr Hacker is a wee bit late. All the clinics have been affected to some degree.'

James Larsson said nothing. Pam Mortimer and all of them could go to hell.

As it was — he'd been there already.

★   ★   ★

In the caféteria that mid-morning the talk was all of the events of the previous night, who did what, who didn't, what system needed to be overhauled, what department procedures needed re-structuring.

And, of course, the stabbed, suspected rapist.

Jean got her coffee and sat talking with two Interns.

One of them said,

'Limbach's pissed off because his secretary's gone missing — probably one prayer too many.'

They chuckled, and collected up their things and waved goodbye.

She looked across the room, bustling with white coated groups and people in sweats. In the far corner Steven was with his team, laughing and joking.

Somehow that made her feel better, rather than wretched. It helped to assuage her guilt about James.

'How you coping, Jean?'

Startled, she found Charles Seigle leaning over her, arm resting on the table. Uncomfortably she said,

'Fine thanks, Charles.'

Seigle dropped his voice, came in a little nearer.

'If you want anything done around the house, or the car — you know you can call on me, don't you?'

'You're very kind.'

Annoyingly, Charles Seigle stayed where he was rather than straighten up.

'There's a crowd of us going to a charity gala performance on Friday — programme's got some *Tosca* and *Madam Butterfly* — I know how much you love opera.

'Would you like to join us?'

She shot a glance at Steven and his group who had just erupted into laughter.

Resentment took over, and an urge to show him that she had a social life too.

'Yes, I would. That's very kind of you all.'

Charles Seigle straightened up.

'Good. I'll pick you up at six.'

Jean regretted it in the instant, stammered,
'Oh, don't worry, I'll find my own way
there.'

Seigle wouldn't hear of it.

'No no — Donald Parsons and Felicity are
coming with me — it's no bother.'

Jean stopped her protests straight away.
With Donald and Felicity in the car that was
all right.

Charles Seigle opened his diary and made
an entry.

'I'll give you a call to remind you if I don't
see you before.'

She tossed some hair out of her eyes as she
said,

'I won't forget.'

★ ★ ★

The steady rise in temperature of the female
changing room for the ER staff finally caused
two maintenance men to be dispatched late
morning. The foreman was in a bad mood.
George Neiminen hadn't been around in days
and wasn't answering his phone.

They knocked on the door, and were
admitted by a middle-aged woman in green
scrubs who called over her shoulder,

'Cover yourself, ladies, the men are here.'

They crossed the room, to the far wall,

161

trying not to look around generally. One set down a tool box as the other erected a set of folding aluminium steps and climbed up, hand feeling in front of the grille.

'Nothing.'

He suddenly looked closer at the grille.

'Hang on, Jim. I think there's something stuck behind it.'

He held out his hand.

'Give me a screwdriver.'

The electric motor of the screwdriver hummed as he drew the bolts out. They came out very easily. His suspicions were aroused.

'What have they done this time.'

He was referring to the students' rag week. Already they'd had to free a stark naked third year from his chains around the founder's statue in the library courtyard. The Dean had already thrown a wobbly over that.

No sooner had he started on the last bolt than it fell out, the grille crashing down on his head as it was pushed from the other side.

He fell sprawling onto the floor, the aluminium ladder clattering the other way. But it was Jim who was rooted to the spot, who yelled the most.

'Oh Jesus.'

A bloodless arm fell out of the black hole, waving from side to side in the sweet smell of human putrefaction.

The woman on the nearest bench seats had come running at the sound of the technician's fall.

They stood in a group, holding hands over their noses and mouths, some tying on surgical masks.

'Those bloody kids have gone too far this time,' choked an older woman.

As they were joined by others she gestured for their benefit.

'They've put a cadaver into the shaft — that's their puny idea of a joke.'

Somebody said — 'It shows a complete lack of respect. Whoever it is should be drummed out of the school — however good they are.'

A fully dressed woman at the back of the little crowd made for the door. 'I'll get the Anatomy Department technicians here.'

The door swung open and closed behind her. Whether it was the rush of air, or just that the body had been delicately balanced and the greasy sheen on the skin helped to lubricate it, but the result was the same.

With a plopping sound like something soft sliding down a plughole, the rest of the body came free as far as the hips, and swung from side to side like a pendulum.

The shock was too much for some of the women, who ran screaming from the room.

But the worst effect was on the older surgeons — the ones who went regularly to the secretaries' floor.

Even with her face upside-down, hair falling around her wide open mouth and eyes bulging, they knew the identity of the head swinging unnaturally before them.

Hanging like something in a butchers' shop, naked, disembowelled, and mutilated, all of them recognized Simon Limbach's secretary —

Marjorie Gooding.

16

'Sorry I'm late.'

Jean apologized as she hurried into the reception of the Neller Wing.

It was a scorchingly hot day already and he had been waiting in the cool, watching the street through the doors, the man on the desk giving him occasional glances.

'No problem.'

She signed him out.

At the car he held the door for her, before he eased himself into the seat beside her. As he fastened his belt she said,

'I'm sorry about tonight, James — Pam has told you I suppose? You've got to be back by six.'

He gave a sheepish grin.

'I never was a good time keeper, Jean.'

The implication wasn't lost on her: excitement mingled with fear.

'Hadn't we better be careful? She is in charge of you clinically. That carries a lot of responsibility — not to mention clout.'

He finished fixing his seat belt, turned slightly the better to see her.

'You leave Pam Mortimer to me. Now

— where are we going?'

Jean put the car into gear and moved off.

'It's such a lovely day I wondered if you'd like to go for a swim.'

When he didn't immediately answer she shot him a sideways glance as she pulled up at the main gates and waited to turn out onto the busy highway.

'No?'

'Sounds just the job, but . . . '

She eased the car forward a foot or two, and braked again.

'But what?'

He gestured with his hand at his chest.

'The scars — they might upset people.'

Jean saw a gap in the traffic, gunned the engine and turned out onto the road.

'Ah, that's where I can surprise you.'

As two police cars, sirens wailing like something portending the end of life on earth passed them going the other way, she said,

'Just you wait and see.'

She glanced in the rear-view mirror, frowning. The police cars had turned into the hospital.

★ ★ ★

Monitoring the police radio traffic, the local reporters were soon at the main entrance, quickly followed by others. Before the day was out TV news crews had taken a few covering shots of the hospital and police activity for a voice-over thirty second slot for that night's early news round-up. A print hack was also a stringer for a syndicate and by mid-afternoon was faxing a lurid account to New York.

The sub-editors were soon getting to work on the hospital connection. Memories were evoked of another man with possible medical connections. Jack the Ripper.

★   ★   ★

'There, what do you think?'

She'd driven almost home, but halfway up the unmade road to her house she turned into the drive of another and down the side to a garage.

They'd walked through a garden gate and out to the back. The blue water of the pool was so still that the sun only reflected off the tiled bottom.

He moved to the edge, settled on his haunches and touched the water before looking up at her.

'All for us?'

She nodded.

'They're away in Europe — open invitation to use it any day.'

He stood up.

'Let's do it.'

Delighted she made to go.

'Right. I'll pop up to the house and get some costumes and towels.'

She was aware as she drove to her house, went in and up the stairs, and got towels from the linen cupboard and a pair of Steven's trunks; knew as she found her own bikini, the green wet-look one that showed off the colour of her skin and hair; and as she got into it and viewed herself in the full length mirror, that she could not deny the growing hunger of her body.

Hastily she drew on a short wrap-around cotton sarong. Fumbling, from the bathroom cabinet she found suntan oils and glasses, then put her feet into a pair of canvas slip-ons.

Nature drove her with a force such that she was barely in control of herself.

Downstairs she went into the kitchen and filled a bag with juice, beers and a couple of glasses.

That was all the time her body would allow.

He was nowhere in sight as she came through the gate. Her heart sank. For a split-second the awful thought struck her that he had gone.

A second rejection so close to Steven's would be crushing.

Then she saw him, moving so deep in the pool that there was no ripple on the surface, legs thrusting, propelling him silently in the depths, arms pushing sideways and up.

Naked.

He reached the end, did a lazy somersault underwater, not breaking the surface, and came back down the length.

Naked. He looked like a Greek god, as he powered along.

She waited.

He touched the end wall, came up, cutting the surface nearly as silently as he had been underneath. Everything he did seemed to be understated — as if you wouldn't know he was there.

'I see you couldn't wait?'

He gave a boyish grin, seemed to be getting younger.

'I figured you'd seen every bit of me when I couldn't do anything about it — so what the hell.'

It was true.

But there was a world of difference away from the hospital.

Something more personal.

Something more — *alive*.

She studiously avoided looking down into

the water beyond his face.

'I guess you're right.'

She unwound the sarong, stepped out of her shoes and dived in over him.

The water roared in her ears, bubbles exploded around her, coming from her mouth.

She came up, broke surface, and took the few strokes that enabled her to reach the end.

Jean did the same turn as he had, and returned half-way under water, before coming up and stopping, her hair floating around her.

'Phew, that's better.'

He swam towards her — on his back.

Jean watched him, eyes drawn to what he had made sure by his choice of stroke that she would see.

Suddenly he rolled over, dived down beneath her, gripping her legs and pushing her upwards.

Jean came out of the water and fell back with a splash. Laughing and playing they cavorted in the water like a couple of children. It lasted for twenty minutes. In the end she got out first, pulling herself up the steps using both handrails.

With towels laid out side by side she lay back on her elbows, chin up, eyes closed to get the sun on her face and neck.

She was like that for several minutes before

he lifted himself effortlessly out of the water and padded silently over to her.

His shadow made her open her eyes. What she saw was a figure towering over her, features lost in the blinding sun behind the head. Then he reached down and the sun freed his face.

James Larsson was smiling.

Not without warmth.

But there was something else.

He reached out and with a delicacy ran his finger down the side of her face and onto her neck.

The words were slow, measured, sincere.

'You are beautiful.'

Jean suddenly unfroze, lifted her arms to lock behind his neck, drew him down onto her.

★ ★ ★

It was only afterwards that she realized the whole thing had been unconsciously engineered by herself.

It had happened on neutral ground, away from the house where she might have felt awkward.

Away from the hospital where it would have been impossible.

Scheming little bitch she thought as she lay

on her side, looking at James Larsson as he dozed. Her eyes took in his body, all scarred and in places discoloured by the torture.

But flesh that was on the mend, skin firmer, muscles hardening with every day that passed.

Flesh that had entered her, driven so deep that it had hurt, a vigorous splendid pain.

It would probably never be like that again, she thought ruefully.

It had reawakened her to life.

⋆　⋆　⋆

The crowd was shocked, voices hushed. In the main lecture room of the Medical School, and overflowing into the corridor outside, they waited to hear Detective Tom O'Hara of the city's police force address them. Wearing a sports jacket and chinos he had thinning grey hair swept straight back, and a small military moustache. His eyes had the weary, cynical look of a man who has seen all of humanity's worst excesses, and nothing would now shock him, and in any case retirement was just two months away.

He brushed the moustache with a curved finger of his left hand and raised his voice.

'Ladies and gentlemen, thank you.'

The room quietened. He cleared his throat. 'You all know the sorry circumstances that

172

bring us together today. I've called this meeting to try to establish some guide lines for us all, because heaven knows, the work load on my officers is going to be bad enough as it is. Apart from investigating the crime we have been asked by the Hospital Management to patrol the buildings for the immediate duration.'

He indicated several uniformed officers at the side doors then picked up a sheet of paper.

'Some calculations have still got to be carried out because of the variable temperatures in the shaft where she was found, but a provisional estimate is that Miss Gooding was killed some twelve hours ago.'

The room filled with talking. O'Hara carried on reading until it subsided. His finger brushed at the moustache.

'So, if any of you saw her immediately prior to that time one of my officers will take your statement. I also want all of you to take one of these forms' — he held up the sheet of paper — 'which will be given to all members of staff. We've set some timings on it which we think are important, so please do your best to give us a complete run-down on your movements in the last twenty-four hours, and of the people you saw — or even think you saw.'

He looked around at the sea of faces.

'We are particularly interested in any sightings of Miss Gooding — anything in the last week even, and of course anyone she was seen talking to — however normal the circumstances. By crosschecking we hope to build up a complete picture of her movements.'

Tom O'Hara waved his hand in what he hoped was the right direction.

'We're setting up a command room in the Medical School itself, thanks to the co-operation of the Dean, and computers will be collating your replies.'

He paused for effect.

'You will also find on the form a phone number.'

He held up the paper and pointed to the bottom right-hand corner.

'This is a confidential line that can be called day and night, if you feel there is anything — *anything* we should know, but is perhaps too delicate for you to approach us directly please — please use it. Anything said will be treated in the strictest confidence. Am I making myself clear?'

'As crystal,' growled Pam Mortimer looking at her watch.

'Anybody can use the line like a poison pen letter.'

O'Hara's voice came again.

'Will you collect your forms now please, as you leave.'

People started to stand up and move towards

the exits, but O'Hara suddenly called out.

'Oh, one other thing.'

They stopped moving. He looked around.

'I know you are all busy people and this is a big hospital with a lot of sick patients who must take priority in your eyes — and quite rightly so.'

He paused for emphasis.

'But this is a *murder* enquiry — make no mistake about that. And if it is necessary to come round to any of your departments in the course of our enquiries, we shall do so.'

He gave a disarming smile.

'Though obviously with the minimum of disturbance. Thank you for your time.'

As the subdued crowd edged down the stairs, the word murder hung heavy in the air.

In the chapel of rest Simon Limbach was on his knees. Tears ran down his face.

For the hundredth time he said a prayer for Marjorie, his good and faithful secretary, a woman of innocence, slaughtered like a sacrificial lamb on the alter of the anti-christ.

He lifted his eyes as the last light of the day filtered through the coloured plastic windows that gave the illusion of stained glass.

Blue and green dappling gave way to dark red on his hands clasped in prayer.

Like blood.

17

It was called *Bruno's*, a restaurant that consisted of one small room turned with Italian flair into something full of character and warmth.

They sat at a table at the back, a secluded recess amongst greenery and terracotta pots, looking at each other over the red-shaded light, glasses of Frascati in their hands.

Jean ran her tongue over her lip.

'I suppose we'd better get back.'

James Larsson sat back.

'Where?'

'To the hospital.'

He played with the edge of his glass on the table, running a finger around its rim. He didn't speak immediately. She grappled with the idea that he might say he wanted to stay the night with her, and decided, yes she would. Everything had happened so quickly, yet she felt happier than she had ever been in her life.

'OK.'

It cut off any such thoughts. Disappointment must have momentarily cast a shadow across her features because he smiled.

'There's plenty of time. We've got the rest of our lives.'

Jean felt a warmth, a contentment. It was, after all the months that had gone before, like coming home into a safe haven.

★   ★   ★

Pam Mortimer was white with anger.

'What the hell do you think you two are doing?'

Jean and Larsson had just walked in to her office, having been directed there by security. She turned to Jean.

'We'll speak again in the morning.'

Jean, initially feeling guilty felt her temper rising, but said quietly,

'It was entirely my fault Pam. I accept full responsibility.'

'You should have known better.'

Jean bit back her reply, said to Larsson,

'I'll see you tomorrow then, James.'

She reached up, and knowing full well that it would shock Pam, gave him a quick kiss.

'Sleep well.'

She turned, gave Pam a look that only women can give each other.

The door closed behind her.

Without another word the psychiatrist moved around and sat at her desk, began writing on a pad of forms, her mouth set in a hard line of bitterness. Her foot found the alarm bell that rang in the units high security section. Immediately two burly attendants dropped what they were doing and raced for the door. It took twenty seconds for them to arrive at Pam Mortimer's office, just as she wrote her signature with a flourish. She looked up at the orderlies, held up the form which one took.

'Take Mr Larsson to room nineteen, would you?'

She turned her attention back to him.

'We'll have to go into your case in greater detail if I'm to help you. We need to control every facet of your life in conditions that we can monitor twenty-four hours a day, seven days a week — you understand? So you will be confined to the unit for now.'

She positively beamed at him.

'Now, as you can see, we are doing everything we can to help you, so I want you to go off with these gentlemen.'

Larsson smiled, stood up, allowed one of the men to hold his arm at elbow and wrist, as if helping him from the chair to the door, only he knew it could be rammed up behind his back at the slightest hint of trouble.

He allowed himself to be gently guided to the door, then suddenly stopped, turned his head, and smiled at the figure behind the desk.

'Good night.'

The door closed out the bleak face of Pam Mortimer.

They walked down the corridor, one white coated attendant on either side, the one on the right still with his two handed grip on wrist and elbow, the one on the left loosely holding his upper arm.

Maybe he wouldn't have done anything then, but the Chinese whispering tinkle came, and the flickering light in his head transformed the corridor into the stonewalls of Afghanistan, a prison that smelt of human excrement and filled with the screams of men dying in torment.

He attacked with ferocious savagery, instantly disabling the one holding him with two hands leaving him clutching his face. His eyes were bulging in a mass of blood where Larsson had jabbed the stiffened fingers of his freed left hand.

As the other leapt onto him he drove his elbow back like a piston into his gut.

Released from the bear hug he picked up a fire extinguisher and finished him off with a swinging blow, then brought instant pain relief to the other with a short jab of the metal base to his head.

Unconscious, the man stopped sobbing.

At the end of the corridor he reached the corner, and peered around it. Below on the main door there were two security men.

Larsson paused, composed himself, then trotted down the stairs, nodding at the men as he made for the doors.

'Just a minute.'

One of them blocked his exit by standing in front of the inswinging glass door.

'Where do you think you're going?'

Innocently Larsson looked across at the man behind the desk, the man with the switches and alarms at his fingertips.

'Out. I've had permission all week, haven't I — part of my therapy. A doctor takes me into town. She's outside waiting.'

The security man at the door was aggressive.

'Cut the shit. Stay over there until we've checked.'

It was the last thing he said for two hours.

Larsson drove a short powerful punch into his gut, grabbed his hair as he doubled up, kneed his face, then spun him around, and drove his defenceless head into a plate-glass door.

Behind him Larsson heard the alarm go. He turned, but the man behind the desk had seen enough. He ran for it.

Outside, he made for the rows of parked vehicles where a couple had just got into their car.

Larsson yanked the driver's door open, snatched the seat belt from the man's hand and gripped his coat, rolling him out onto the tarmac. He jumped in.

A woman sat frozen in the passenger seat as he drove slowly away down the long drive to the highway and pulled into the sidewalk.

Gently he said,

'You get out here.'

Without a word she did as she was told. In the rear view mirror he noticed she just stood there dazed, not rushing to get help, not doing anything.

He drove off into the night.

18

Lieutenant Tom O'Hara was at home when the call came through. It was Detective Sergeant Rhew whom he knew to be a reliable fellow of Chinese extraction.

He took the empty pipe from his mouth as he listened, hoping it was news of the hospital engineer, one George Nieminen who seemed to have disappeared, and who was now the prime suspect for the murder of Marjorie Gooding.

The man who had been stabbed by the vigilante — if that's what he was — had been temporarily ruled out for the moment, not because of his denial of any involvement, but because there was as yet no DNA evidence, or anything else, to implicate him.

Besides, what had been done to Marjorie was horrendous, and required some knowledge of surgery said the Medical Examiner. O'Hara grunted. Maybe this Nieminen guy, working at the hospital, had picked up the idea, read books, heard the students talking or had seen things. Who knew.

Still, rapists were one thing, homicidal butchery another.

But it was not news of Nieminen.

A violent mental patient had severely wounded three people before commandeering a car and driving off.

'You think it's possible that this man could be involved with the murder of Miss Gooding?'

Rhew told him that the consultant psychiatrist, one Pam Mortimer, couldn't rule out the possibility. The man had been free to wander the hospital before they'd realized he was so dangerous, some sort of soldier back from the war. Been through a lot — they had been doing a case assessment.

O'Hara tapped the cold stem on his cheek as Rhew continued.

'He's been friendly with a woman, sir — her name is Dr Jean Hacker.'

'I see. Does this Dr Mortimer think she is in danger?'

'Says it's likely that he will certainly seek her out — he knows where she lives. Shall I get a car to call up there, sir, we have an address?'

'Yes, better safe than sorry. See if the Hacker family want somebody there all night, if they do, set it up. Oh, and Rhew . . . '

'Sir?'

'Get onto the soldier's unit. We'll need to know more about him for ourselves. What's his name?'

'James Larsson. Seems he's with Special Forces — Dr Hacker has taken him to her home. They walked in the forest there apparently, something to do with his treatment. He doesn't know anybody in the city, sir, so it's my guess he'll go back to her area.'

O'Hara's voice suddenly hardened.

'In that case, soon as we can, set up a surveillance detail on the Hacker household, irrespective of whether we have a car stationed there to begin with, and we may need to think about searching that forest if he stays missing — get onto the Park Rangers.'

O'Hara said goodnight, switched off his cell, and went back into the lounge. Mrs O'Hara sat with her Yorkshire Terrier on her lap, knitting, watching NCIS on the television.

'Everything all right, dear?'

O'Hara grunted, knowing a real reply was not required.

But he *was* troubled, remembering again the look of Marjorie Gooding's mortal remains and the awful things that had been done to her. It was the work of a madman, with no sense of pity.

OK, lines of investigation were underway delving into the victim's background, looking for anyone with a motive.

But this was no 'ordinary' crime of passion, of that he was certain.

This son of a bitch was a deranged maniac.

Tom O'Hara scratched his moustache.

Where all the extra manpower was coming from, if this affair got out of hand, God only knew. It was a hell of a big hospital, a city within the city. If fear got a grip he might end up having to plead with his boss to go to the Governor for more resources. Computers would make a difference of course, were already at work cross-checking the files of the FBI, looking for any murder in the last ten years where the victim had been tortured and dissected in a particularly obscene way.

And what had been done to her took time, and a very quiet, very secure set-up.

He shuddered.

A torture chamber in fact.

★ ★ ★

Jean was angry — so angry with Pam Mortimer that she was shaking as she drove home.

The woman was jealous, it was so obvious, but the really awful thing was she was using her medical clout to break them up and restrict James to the hospital. It was so unethical, so unfair.

185

She was brought back from her rage by the scream of tyres and the piercing blast of a truck horn.

Jean fought the wheel as she over-reacted and put her car into a broadside skid until it came to a halt. Only then was it clear to her what had happened. In her blind rage she had jumped an intersection, had driven in front of an articulated truck.

In her rear mirror she could see the driver getting down from his cab.

It was just too much. Law abiding Jean Hacker drove off, shakily turning the corner. Half a mile down the road was a fast food place. She turned in, got herself a coffee.

If she went on like this, she'd end up killing somebody.

End up dead herself.

She took her time, waited until the heat had gone from her body before she got back into the car and continued her drive home.

Jean went from anger to one of almost light heartedness. James Larsson, the most unlikely man in terms of background that she could ever have imagined, had stirred something in her that she had not known she had possessed.

It was the obvious contrast between them she supposed. James exuded a masculine toughness, yet there was that underlying vulnerability — an irresistible combination to any woman. She knew instinctively, that without a doubt he needed her as much as she needed him.

There were no half feelings. It was all or nothing. It happened sometimes, to some people she conceded. Like molecules of hydrogen finding one of oxygen.

Jean chuckled at her analogy.

That was an explosive reaction, ironically giving water — and water was a prerequisite for life.

Something in her womb stirred at the thought.

Jean turned into the drive, decided to park outside, and not bother with the garage.

Later, in her bedroom she did something she'd never done before in her life, at least, not in the way she did now. Naked, she looked at herself in a full length mirror and blushed at the realization.

She was checking to see what James had seen.

Shaking her head in disbelief, she went to the back of the bedroom door for her nightie.

It wasn't on the hook.

Nor was it under the pillow.

Shrugging she selected a new one and got into bed. Although she couldn't remember, she must have popped it into the washing machine that morning.

Down in the dark utility room the washing machine was empty.

In the bright moonlight at the end of the garden, the trees creaked and groaned in the swirls of warm air, accompanied by the flapping noise of the silk nightie tied by the shoulder straps to one of the branches.

It had been slashed to ribbons.

19

'There it is.'

The Patrol Sergeant pointed through the window of the police car as they reached the top of the hill. The house was in darkness, a car parked outside.

'It looks as if they've gone to bed. Check with HQ — see if they want us to disturb them.'

They did.

The police car turned into the drive and the sergeant got out. Armed with a clipboard he shone his flashlight on the bell, pushed it and held it for several seconds. It rang deep in the dark house.

Jean was already asleep when the noise brought her back to consciousness. Quickly she drew on her dressing-gown, paused to look down through her window. The sight of the police car startled her. The truck driver must have seen her registration number.

Her heart sank as she tripped down the stairs unbolted the door and opened it.

A large police officer stood there, apologetic.

'Sorry to trouble you, ma'am — is your husband in?'

Jean found herself repeating him like an idiot.

'Husband?'

'Yes. Dr J Hacker?'

It was not his fault that the message contained no directions as to the sex.

Jean shook her head. 'No, that's me.'

The police officer shrugged.

'Sorry, they didn't make that clear, Doctor. The point is a patient has escaped from the psychiatric wing at the hospital and could be a danger to you.'

Jean was rooted to the spot, trying to take it all in.

'Patient?'

The police sergeant glanced at his board.

'Yes, somebody called Larsson. Would that mean anything to you?'

Jean started to think on her feet.

Pam — it must be something that that woman had done.

'Oh him — he's no real problem. If he turns up here we'll make him a coffee and bring him back in the morning.'

The police officer eyed her suspiciously.

'It says here he's inflicted injury on three people who tried to stop him.'

Instinct made her react firmly.

'Then they mishandled him, it's a disgrace.'

The police officer frowned.

'Perhaps I ought to speak to your husband — just to be sure.'

Jean now grasped what to do. She *wanted* James Larsson to come to her, to seek refuge with her.

For ever.

It was paramount that this police officer did not find out she was alone.

'That won't be necessary, Sergeant, I'm quite capable of speaking for us both. Now, if that's all I'll bid you goodnight. Both of us have heavy schedules in the morning.

'Very good, ma'am. Please be sure all windows and doors are secure.'

He touched his finger to his cap in a relaxed salute, 'Goodnight.'

Thanking him, she closed the door before he had gone a few feet down the drive, leaning back on it, heart racing.

What could she do?

The only thing she could think of was to put on some downstairs lights as soon as the police car had gone. It would tell him she was up — ready, waiting.

She turned out the lights, ran up the stairs, turned out the bedroom ones and went to the window. The police car was turning. If they were still watching the place they would see normal signs of a household that had gone back to sleep, untroubled by any thoughts of a missing patient.

The sergeant buckled himself in and reached for the radio.

'Well, there's one laid back household for you.'

Jean watched the car drive away and let the curtain drop back into place. In the darkness she sat waiting, heart thumping, knowing nothing of the fate of poor Marjorie Gooding.

★   ★   ★

She woke with a start around two o'clock, and came forward in the chair, disorientated for a moment. Jean looked at her watch, wondered why at 2 a.m. she was downstairs, and then it all came back to her.

She glanced around. Had there been a noise? Jean got up, went to the front door.

It was a warm night, the light wind had dropped and thick white mist had formed, lying like a low blanket in the trees.

Insects zig-zagged in the porchlight as she turned it on.

'James?'

It sounded daft, saying it out loud, but she half expected him to appear — moving out of the trees.

'James?'

Nothing but the insects moved.

She closed the door.

The kitchen was in darkness. She flicked on the light. It spasmed in the fluorescent tubes before it stayed on, harsh and unrelenting. She heated the kettle, waited, finally taking a cup of hot chocolate to bed.

Disappointment came welling up. It seemed in his hour of need, he hadn't turned to her.

But out of the white mist there had come a figure — one dressed all in black, its head covered by a black woollen balaclava from which the slanted eyes, hard and glittering, surrounded by haloes of white crinkled skin, caught the reflection of the moon's image. It halted, stood as unmoving as the trees for minutes on end. A moth descended on the face, stayed there, its wings opening and closing.

It was ten minutes before Jean suddenly passed the bedroom window. The figure jerked, the moonlight flashing on the blood stained knife in its black gloved hand. The moth flew away.

But the sinister creature of the night had the power of human thought and human evil.

There was time, plenty of time now that she was alone to do things right — to enjoy it to the full. There would be no need to use the hidey-hole — this house was secure and

193

isolated. Her screams would only echo down the empty dark corridors of the forest.

Soon — very soon.

The saliva ran in its mouth. It opened, an obscene red gash against the black.

The moon was slowly obscured by a cloud. The light dimmed, the wood became black.

When it rode free again the creature was gone.

20

Jean was staggered by the massive police presence as she drove into the hospital. What on earth had happened when he'd got free? A sense of doom gripped her. She hurriedly parked the car at Neller Wing, eager to get at Pam Mortimer.

There was a police officer at the entrance to the Department of Psychological Medicine. She noticed that the door was boarded up on one side. The plate glass pieces had been swept up, but bits remained at the edge of the sidewalk.

She made to go in but a policeman stopped her.

'Sorry — its not open to the public yet.'

Colour came into her cheeks as she rummaged in her purse for her ID.

She held it up.

'I'm staff — Doctor Hacker. I have patients.'

The police officer's jaw dropped. He'd never seen such a good looking doctor in his life.

'Sorry ma'am, but there's a forensic team in there at the moment. One of the inmates cut up rough and got away. It's probable that he had something to do with the murder.'

Jean actually swayed. Murder, my God, they hadn't told her last night about a murder.

'He killed somebody?' she croaked.

It was the policeman's turn to look at her strangely.

'Yes.'

'Somebody actually saw him do it?'

He shrugged.

'Well, no. The woman was found in the main hospital — a secretary, Goodman I think her name was.'

'Gooding.'

'Yeah — that's it.'

Jean felt physically sick.

She mumbled something the police officer took to be 'thank you', but he was distracted as she walked away by a burst of static and a voice from his lapel radio.

He leaned his head to one side and pressed the transmit button.

'One nine three receiving.'

Jean went to the main hospital, found it was like a building under seige. All the doors were guarded by police, and she was stopped again as she tried to enter.

'Have you had one of these?'

A young police officer held out the form

Detective O'Hara had asked them all to fill in. She took it, reading as she walked along the corridor.

There was a brief summary, with the timings as O'Hara had promised. Jean's mind raced back, tried to think of where she had been.

Where *he* was.

But she just knew it was not James.

The 'prep' room was strangely quiet, with no nurses bustling around. In fact there was nobody at all.

A faint padding came from behind. She turned to say good morning: There was no one there.

She actually felt the hair on her scalp prickle.

'Hello?' Her voice echoed in the tiled room. Perhaps the noise had been the air-conditioning. But it was strange — why wasn't there at least somebody around by now?

The emptiness, the stillness of what should have been a busy unit beginning to wind up for the day's activities began to frighten her. Jean moved to the double doors leading into the OR. She looked through the windows. Nobody was in sight, the operating table starkly empty, the banks of electronic instruments surrounding it lifeless, the

197

monitoring screens blank.

She made for the doors leading back out to the corridor and looked through the small observation portal.

It loomed long and empty, distorted by the wide angle lens of the glass so that the next double doors looked tiny, set at the end of a corridor stretching away as if in a surreal film.

Empty.

The noise came again, a peculiar shuffling.

The *killer* — he was in here, with her — had been hidden all night.

The fear burst in her like a bomb. Jean dropped everything, ran blindly, running for the doors at the other end of the corridor. Her outstretched hands tensed for the impact. At the moment of touch the door caved inwards. Screaming, Jean Hacker felt herself falling into a yawning pit of horror. At the end was a huge figure in scrubs and a cap, eyes dramatic against a strange blackness —

And something flashed in his hand.

★ ★ ★

Detective Tom O'Hara was up early. He'd had a restless night, finding the increasingly oppressive weather difficult to sleep in, even with the bedroom windows open.

Not that he would have been able to sleep

198

anyway. He strolled down the neat concrete path, to his greenhouse.

Tom O'Hara liked it in there, always had, the smell of the peat, the colour of the earthenware pots, the seedlings, the tomatoes.

He liked it more than ever now, since it was the only place he could enjoy a quiet contemplative pipe. He packed in his favourite tobacco, lit up, sat down on the stool in the corner, and sucked in the glorious fumes.

His mind turned to this current murder case — undoubtedly his last before he retired.

He didn't like it. O'Hara grunted, took his mouth from the stem, and blew out some smoke.

When did he ever like murder? But he knew what he meant. There was a 'funny feel' about this one.

Of course, it could all end suddenly if this soldier turned out to be their man. And that seemed more than likely.

He sucked contentedly again at the pipe, enjoying the rich taste.

The Regional Crime Lab had promised to expedite the remaining tests — if overtime payments were allowed.

He grunted. *Money.* The love of it was the root of all evil so they said. But in his experience evil was quite able to thrive without the help of anything.

— Except man.

His wife's voice floated out of the house down the garden and into his little world.

'Tom, don't forget to put that thing out before you come in for breakfast.'

He tapped the pipe on his heel.

— Or women.

★ ★ ★

Jean's scream ended with the crashing of steel trays and breaking glass on the tiled floor. In the intense silence after the noise subsided, she looked up into the eyes, big frightened eyes, white against the black skin of the technician.

'Are you all right, doctor?'

With a supreme effort she got herself together, and nodded.

He dropped to his knees. 'Looks as though these specimen tubes are a goner.'

She put her hand to her forehead.

'I'm sorry . . . I . . . shouldn't have been running. I thought I heard something.'

He began to pick up the pieces.

'That's all right. I can get most of these replaced before surgery — I was half an hour ahead of schedule.'

Stunned, she looked at her watch. Understanding began to dawn in Jean Hacker as the violent storm of panic subsided. She was nearly an hour early.

But her pulse remained high, reminded her of the terror that only seconds before had coursed through her on a shock wave of adrenalin.

She never discovered what the noise was, and had recovered sufficiently in time to start the session without embarrassment. She consoled herself that she had only reacted instinctively.

Nature's way — fight or flight.

And she had taken flight.

Because that was the only sane thing to do — from an insane killer.

★   ★   ★

It was eleven o'clock when the blonde girl found the printed note in her pigeon hole. It simply said, 'See me in the Path. Office at six.' It wasn't signed, but she knew who it must be from.

She looked around, made sure nobody had seen it, then screwed it up and put it in a bin.

As she left she checked her friend's pigeon hole. There was no note there. Maybe Mary had picked hers up already. Annabel smiled. Somehow though, she had a feeling Seigle had only wanted her, after all, she did the *most* for him. Besides, it would look better if she and Mary didn't get identical exam results.

She went to the rest room, came out and washed her hands, checking her appearance in the wall mirror. Not bad, it would certainly do for old Seigle.

She fiddled with her hair, straightened the elastic belt that pulled in her small waist even more, and smoothed out the suede mini with the palm of her hand.

She picked up her books and note pad, and slung her small red bag over her shoulder. But first — there was anatomy dissection. She went into the room with its sixty odd cadavers covered with white sheets, and its familiar smell of formaldehyde. Her class occupied one half of the room, the other was always the year below them. Not that there was much left of the bodies on her side. The sheets had a decided hollow look about them. Because of course, they were eighteen months ahead, and the cadavers were nearly finished.

She noted out of the corner of her eye that a new body was lying under its cover in the no man's land between the two sides of the room.

There could be no question but that it was one that would be dissected by the staff for examination purposes.

* ★ ★

At the same time Detective Tom O'Hara sat down in the small area designated for 'conferences'.

Beside him was Sergeant John Rhew, broad shouldered, short hair, inscrutable Chinese face, whilst opposite, opening a very thin file he'd just taken from his briefcase was a man with a neat little beard, rimless glasses and a large adam's apple: the Medical Examiner.

The man had extensive photographs in front of him. He pushed them across the table.

'You know the nature of the injuries to her I believe, Detective?'

O'Hara waved the pipe stem like a conductor's batton.

'The semen — have you got a blood match from it yet?'

'There was no semen.'

O'Hara looked at him in astonishment.

'No semen, *anywhere*?'

The doctor kept on shaking his head. 'None in any orifice — vagina, anal, oral. I even checked what was left of her cleavage — nothing.'

'So you are telling me that he used a condom?'

The ME shrugged.

'It's certainly possible. But of course there were massive injuries inflicted afterwards.'

O'Hara noticed that Sergeant Rhew, a man to have with you on any Saturday night patrol, was looking decidedly green. He had a young wife.

The man with the goatee beard cleared his throat.

'I can add to your discomfort I'm afraid, Superintendent.'

O'Hara scowled.

'Go on.'

'We found no traces of human hair, blood, sweat, semen, saliva, urine or skin cells on her.'

'*None?*'

The man emphasized his answer with a single sideways shake of his head.

'Nope, except — '

'Fingernails?'

O'Hara had seen them for himself and had wondered.

'Yes. That's the one area where we had some success. They were torn and bleeding, and under all of them we found old stone and . . . '

He tweezered out a tiny bit of fibre from a plastic bag and held it up to view.

'What is that?'

'A form of fungus you find in sewers and dark moist places, that sort of thing.'

O'Hara and Rhew exchanged glances. So the killer had found a place where he'd kept her before torturing her to death.

O'Hara's back ached as he asked,

'How do you account for the total lack of body evidence?'

The goatee beard received a stroke from its owner.

'Barrier nursing is the nearest thing I can think of.'

O'Hara leaned forward.

'How do you mean?'

'Well, he must have used a gown, surgical gloves, mask, cap, everything you'd get in a hospital.'

His voice faltered, died away as he realized the implication of what he'd said as suddenly as all the rest of them.

O'Hara nervously rubbed at the bowl of his cold pipe.

'So you're saying he's not so much an outsider as a member of the staff?'

'Not necessarily, but he had access to everything he needed, knew how to use it, so . . .'

Sergeant Rhew said, 'Could this fellow Nieminen, the maintenance man, have picked it up from what he regularly saw?'

The man shrugged.

'Your guess is as good as mine. He would

certainly have access to the stuff he needed.'

Sergeant Rhew glanced at his chief.

'He's missing from his place, sir, shall I apply for a search warrant?'

Almost absent mindedly O'Hara nodded. He was thinking more of the violent mental patient. Could he still be in the hospital? And would he have the savvy to leave no trace of himself on the victim? After all, his trade was violence, and more to the point, probably *knew* that in this day and age, more than ever before in the history of violent, unlawful death, there must be no trace of the perpetrator on his victim if the former were to remain undetected.

Maybe they were taught such techniques for covert missions? The thought excited him enough to make a note to enquire of the powers-that-be to find out.

Aggression, training and *madness* — an unholy trinity.

21

Eyes blazing, Jean leaned over Pam Mortimer's desk thumping it with her fist.

'What the hell do you think you are doing? Half the police force in the city are looking for James, thanks to you.'

The psychiatrist looked angrily back at her.

'I might ask you the same — in fact I could have you struck off for what you've done.'

Such a threat twenty-four hours ago would have devastated Jean, would have brought her up in mid-flight, drained her anger with worry. Because there *were* grounds — professional misconduct. But twenty-four hours ago was somebody else's lifetime, and if Pam Mortimer hoped for an apology from Jean she was to be disappointed.

Jean stormed.

'Don't insult my intelligence, Pam — you are just jealous — its written all over your face.'

Pam Mortimer leapt up.

'How dare you say that. I needed help from a colleague and look what I got instead. What you did was intolerable.'

Jean's lips curled back in distaste.

'Intolerable? I didn't think you would be interested in a real man.'

The psychiatrist lashed out, caught Jean across the cheek with a stinging blow with the flat of her hand.

Jean lost her balance, fell sideways by the desk, and hit her head on the corner. She was still overcome with shock and dizziness when Pam Mortimer came around and started laying into her on the floor, beating at her with her fists.

As Jean kicked out and came up onto her feet the woman seemed to take hold of herself, stepped back, clutching at the desk for support before she staggered away and slumped into her chair.

There was silence for a moment as they took stock of themselves. Pam Mortimer pulled some tissues from a box and pressed them to her eyes as Jean felt the skin of her cheek, and the weal that was already forming. But there was only one thing uppermost in her mind.

'There was no call to do to James Larsson what you did. He's very vulnerable.'

The psychiatrist looked shattered and seemed to have shrunk in stature, her assuredness gone.

She folded the tissue, found a dry section.

'I know. I'll do all I can to help. I'll see the

detective in charge, say I overreacted.'

She looked down into her lap.

'I'm sorry it has come to this.'

Jean picked up the telephone, held it out to her, her voice icy.

'Do what you say you will, Pam.'

★ ★ ★

Tom O'Hara was back in his greenhouse when the call came through on his cell.

He snapped into it.

'Yes, O'Hara here.'

It was the good and faithful Rhew. Tom O'Hara had already observed the young man's hard work and commonsense.

'Sir, sorry to trouble you at home, but I've just had a very apologetic Doctor Mortimer on the phone. Seems she now says the patient who escaped last night is quite incapable of a *sexually* motivated murder. Says she overreacted — has been under a lot of stress lately. Thought you ought to know . . . '

His voice tailed off as he wondered what the boss was going to say.

O'Hara's moustache lifted at one side as his lip curled up. He'd had a lifetime of psychiatrists' 'help'. The worst occasion was when a double child-killer had been allowed out on parole on the advice of one of them:

the doors of the high security prison had opened at ten o'clock in the morning. The man stabbed a boy of nine to death in the afternoon.

'Thank you, Sergeant. Well, that may be the case, but when we get him he'll still have to jump through the hoop like anybody else.'

Rhew said, 'About Dr Hacker. Do you still want us to set up the surveillance on her house? I asked Doctor Mortimer's advice and she said she thought it completely unnecessary.'

Tom O'Hara was already having budget problems. He took a deep breath.

'Yes — let it run tonight until I see this Doctor Mortimer in the morning. By then we might have got him.'

'You still want the forest around the house searched, sir?'

Since it involved men already rostered and the National Guard were taking a large share at no extra cost to their budget, O'Hara said, 'Yes', just as his wife called out 'Supper's ready.'

Before Tom O'Hara cut the connection, Rhew said quickly,

'That leaves George Nieminen. Still no trace of him, sir.'

O'Hara's lips pressed firmly together. 'I know.'

Annabel finished her coffee and pushed it away from her. There were eight of them from her year, all grouped around a rectangular table in the cafeteria, their bottles, glasses, plates and cups scattered its surface.

'I'm off,' she said.

There was some backchat from the boys present, young men with great powers of imbibing not only the golden liquid, but literally thousands of scientific facts on the human body as a 'machine' — its engineering and function.

But as yet they had no experience of tampering with that 'machine'. When they went 'clinical' in a couple of months time, the ones who would make good in their chosen career would soon become apparent. For the art of doctoring was not given to all, nor could it be obtained by just studious bookwork. The human body was more than a machine.

Mary was surprised, reached quickly for her coke.

'Hold on, I haven't finished.'

Annabel had had all afternoon to think of her excuse — knew it had to be firm.

She put a hand on Mary's shoulder holding her down as she was about to rise.

'I've got a late appointment with the Admin. Secretary about my state funding. I'll see you back at the house. Bye.'

She left, striding purposefully to the double doors only a few feet away. Once through she looked back. Mary hadn't come through the door. Annabel stopped then, and went in a different direction, down the stairs to the tunnel that led to Seigle's office. The sound of her heels echoed off walls.

When the tunnel turned at an angle of forty-five degrees, she was the only one in the section. The medical school departments were running down for the day, not like the hospital that went on working, twenty-four hours a day, seven days a week, fifty-two weeks of the year. She went past the dissecting rooms and found Seigle's office.

Instinctively she flicked at her hair, undid the top button of her blouse as she negotiated a big used linen trolley parked along the tunnel wall, and knocked on the door. Normally, with anyone else of the faculty, she would have waited, but with Seigle she felt they were on equal terms — business partners in fact. She pushed the door open and went in.

It was empty. Frowning she checked her watch.

Deliberately she'd left it late, just to make sure he was sweating a little.

There was a creaking and shuffling sound behind her, from the direction of the tunnel.

She turned.

Seeming to fill the whole doorway was a figure dressed in surgical green gown with a complete hood of the type used by orthopaedic and neurosurgeons, and a mask. Only his eyes were showing, strange, piercing and full of *desire*.

Her hand went to her throat.

'My God, you frightened me.'

The figure remained motionless.

Annabel slipped her bag off her shoulder and let it fall to the floor, set her notes on the desk beside her and said sarcastically,

'All right, is it doctors and patients time?'

And then when he still didn't move, when those strange eyes continued to bore into her, Annabel suddenly remembered the world beyond herself and the examinations.

The madman — the *murderer*.

'It' saw that she *knew*. In the split second before he leapt forward she turned, hand stretched out to the desk phone. She got to it.

One arm reached around her waist, lifted her kicking and screaming into the air. The other hand clamped around her nose and mouth, a grip of unrelenting iron — in his gloved hand there was a throat-pack soaked in chloroform.

She clawed desperately at the rubber-gloved hand, feet kicking back at his legs.

They struck home, again and again without result, until her shoes flew off.

It took over a minute until her feet stilled. Then she was taken to the laundry basket and dumped into it like a rag doll. As 'it' went back and replaced the phone, picking up her shoes and purse and throwing them on top of her, the hooded figure seemed eerily indifferent, its movements were mechanical as it drew sheets over her inert form, and then slowly wheeled the trolley away.

Annabel was beginning her short ride to an underground part of the Medical School she had never seen, never knew existed, a room from 1812 when the first medical school had been founded.

Only Marjorie Gooding had been there before her in the last one hundred odd years. The silent hooded figure worked swiftly, making sure she was secure, its shadow on the old stone wall, like a medieval monk, at prayer.

22

Jean wondered if James would be at the house when she got home, and actually stood in the drive before she opened the front door, looking around.

The police officer in the surveillance team on the edge of the forest watched through field glasses, whistling under his breath in appreciation. The radio standing by his colleague was turned down, so that its squawk would not give them away.

He knew that at the back of the house, another surveillance team was hiding in the trees at the bottom of the garden. One of them had taken down a tattered strip of woman's underclothing that had got in the way of their observations.

But Jean was disappointed. There was no sign of him. The silence in the house was oppressive. The after-shock of the fight with Pam Mortimer began to set in. Her hands were trembling as she poured a stiff brandy. Its fiery sting made her shudder, but it seemed to have the desired effect.

She slumped into an easy chair, kicked off her shoes and triggered the television with the remote, but paid no attention to the latest news of events in Afghanistan or Israel.

All she wanted was for him to come to her. Exhausted, she finally went to sleep, legs curled up under her, the empty glass dropping from her fingers onto the soft carpet.

★ ★ ★

By nine o-clock that night Mary was very worried. Annabel hadn't come back to the house they shared. The trouble was, in her heart of hearts she knew that her friend was up to something. All that stuff about her finances was a load of crap. She *was* with Dr Seigle.

Anger and frustration finally give way to worry. She grabbed her coat and headed for the hospital.

She scurried along the empty dimly-lit tunnel to his room. The door was closed.

With desperation welling up in her she gripped the handle, took a deep breath, and walked in.

The office was almost totally dark.

'Annabel?'

Her voice was shrill with anxiety.

Mary found the light switch, flicked it on. She half expected to see them caught in the act and would have welcomed it at that moment. Instead there was only the desk, books, all the usual things.

Disappointed, she turned to go then saw the telephone. Quickly she closed the door, sat on the desk and dialled for an outside line.

They all knew where Seigle lived — had visited the large old house called Chimneys when he entertained students with end-of-term drinks parties. She knew the number. Mary dialled, her finger stabbing quickly on the buttons.

She looked around, frightened in the cold emptiness, surrounded only by parts of the dead.

The line connected, began its muted purr. It seemed to go on for ever, then, 'Dr Seigle.'

'Annabel's there — isn't she?'

There was a pause then his voice asked.

'Who is this?'

'Annabel's there — let me speak to her.'

There was another hesitation, before,

'Mary, is that you? What's the matter?'

She told him.

His voice was defensive, frightened.

'Well she's not here.'

Mary twisted the cord of the telephone.

'Oh God, something terrible has happened to her, I know it. I've got to tell the police.

There's a murderer loose in this place.'

'*Wait* — if you do that they'll question you, everything we've done will come out. It will finish us both.'

Mary started to cry. 'What am I going to do then — I've got to do something?'

'Let me think. Where are you?' He sounded desperate.

'In your office.'

'Good. Stay there. I'll get changed and come to you straight away. We'll talk it through. Give me fifteen minutes.'

Unseen, she shook her head.

'They've got to know she's missing.'

'Yes, of course. I'll go with you — it will add weight — otherwise they might think its part of a student prank or something.'

She let out a sob.

'Mary, have you told anyone about us?'

'No, not yet.'

He sounded relieved.

'There's no need to do that at all. We'll work something out. Wait for me — O.K.?'

'Very well, but hurry.'

Hand shaking she slammed the phone down.

Petrified, Mary sat in the silence of the night. Then, as she waited, listening for Seigle's footsteps, she heard a shuffling sound, and the squeak of a wheel on a trolley moving slowly in the tunnel.

Some instinct, a deep felt terror made her flick off the light and shrink down behind his desk into the dark.

★ ★ ★

Annabel was in pitch blackness. Eyes and mouth taped, she was spreadeagled on some sort of bench.

She'd stopped screaming, it only filled the inside of her head. Now she seemed to be drifting in limbo.

And limbo was a place between everlasting life — and death.

Between heaven — and *hell*.

★ ★ ★

In the dark depths of the forest, James Larsson, face blacked and streaked with earth, moved without sound, stopping frequently, listening, smelling.

Eventually he reached the foot of the escarpment and stood among the ferns where he had been with Jean.

Pushing the fronds aside he sank down, scooping at the fine soft soil. When the shallow trough was deep enough he took two plastic garbage bags that he had found in a back street from his pocket. He lined the hole with one, lay down on it, and put the other over him. Starting with his feet he brought the mounds of soil over his body.

Finally only his face remained, and one arm. He gently closed the ferns back around him.

From less than a foot away there was no trace of the man who had sank down there ten minutes before.

Larsson began to feel secure, and warm — a warmth that rose out of Mother Earth — through his body, into his soul, a primordial communion with nature: succour for a wounded animal.

He closed his eyes, and sleep came — for the first time dreamless.

For there are no dreams in the grave.

★   ★   ★

By morning the police officers on surveillance were stiff and tired. One was sitting with his legs outstretched to balance himself as, with hands behind his neck, he did some callisthenics to try and get the blood going again.

The radio crackled. His colleague lowered his glasses and reached for it, flicked up the volume as he sat on a tree trunk.

'Receiving, over.'

The voice crackled back at them.

'Jim, the dog teams and National Guard will be starting their sweep in fifteen minutes, coming from the top end. Should be with you in an hour.'

'Jesus, about time,' was the reply.

The figure crouching near them tensed at the word, 'dog'.

As silently as he had come, the figure withdrew.

Directly he was out of range Larsson began to run, covering the ground in long strides, eyes searching for the one place where he could hide from trained man-hunting dogs.

He found it.

It took time, he was only just finishing as a German Shepherd burst into the glade, carried on past, then came back to the tree, barking and jumping up its trunk, red tongue hanging from a dark muzzle.

A handler came into view.

'What is it, boy?'

He looked around for any sign of footprints. There were none, then up the tree. He could see nothing.

He called to another handler moving fifty yards away.

'Bill. Give us a hand here will you?'

The blue coveralled officer, wearing field boots joined him, bent down so that the first man put his foot on his cupped hands and gave him a lift.

The police officer caught the lowest branch, swung himself up, then climbed higher to another branch and stood on it, looking further up the tree. He could see nothing suspicious. But the dog, joined by the one from the other handler continued to bark.

At that moment the line of troops in berets and camouflaged fatigues, with the odd dark uniform of the police came through the shrubbery, stabbing and thrashing into it with long sticks.

As the line drew level a whistle blew, and a police sergeant came across.

'Anything?'

'No.'

They quietened the dogs.

'Could have been a squirrel.'

The man in the tree swung down, held onto the lower branch, then dropped to the fern covered ground.

'He may have been here though, and made a break for it.'

The sergeant used his hand held transmitter to inform search HQ, then blew twice on his whistle again. The line continued its advance, pushed its way out of sight.

Nothing moved in the glade, except the

odd bird, one of which settled on James Larsson, singing for all its worth. Finally it splashed him with droppings before flying off.

His head, covered in ferns faced skywards, his feet stood on a branch, body lashed to the thinning trunk near the top of the tree. Strips of cloth, twigs and ferns camouflaged his shape and made it impossible to see him from below.

If they had been the enemy he would have reported their position, movement, and numbers, or killed the officers with a silenced rifle; or both.

As it was he just waited.

He gave it a long time before he cut himself free, dropping lightly to earth. Crouching, he went straight into the undergrowth, following the line of the beaters.

An hour later he watched as they all climbed into their trucks and drove away. And the police cars and the surveillance teams.

Soon he was left alone again with the woods.

And Jean's house.

★   ★   ★

Seigle was brought in to see Tom O'Hara, who looked up from his desk.

'You want to see me about something urgently?'

Seigle couldn't look him in the eyes.

'You said everything will be in the strictest confidence?'

Rhew, who was leaning against a radiator, straightened up — suddenly alert.

O'Hara reached for his empty pipe. Here it comes he thought. Guilt was stamped all over this man's face.

'I'll guarantee that anything you say that doesn't have to be used in a court of law will be kept strictly between ourselves, Doctor — unless of course what you tell me is a breach of the law itself.'

Seigle sat in silence for a moment, the defeat written in the way his large frame was slumped in the chair. Then it all came with a rush.

He told them everything, except for the more bizarre details of the sex he had had with both girls at once.

O'Hara listened until Seigle paused at the point where he'd received Mary's call.

'So, you're saying that this medical student, Annabel, has gone missing?'

Seigle shook his head.

'No, worse than that, when I got to my office there was no sign of Mary either.'

Sergeant Rhew raised an eyebrow.

'*Two* women. It must be a student joke.'

Seigle twisted around to face him, then

turned back to O'Hara.

'Don't you understand — something terrible has happened.'

Rhew came to the table, leaned over him, face hard.

'You're saying they're dead?'

Seigle exploded.

'How the hell should I know — you're the police — you tell me, but there has been one murder here already. What the hell does it look like to you?'

In the silence, unthinking, Tom O'Hara snapped open his lighter and stared at the flame.

This man's news was frightening.

★   ★   ★

Jean called Pam Mortimer, barking down the line as soon as she heard the latter's voice, 'I thought you were speaking to the police about James?'

'I did. The police are concentrating on Nieminen now — the hospital is alive with the rumour he was seen in the nurses' block on more than one occasion when he shouldn't have been there.'

Jean pressed her lips together in a firm line.

'Is that so? Well, I can tell you that the National Guard has just been swarming all over the woods here — so they seem to be very much after James.'

'But, Jean, you were there when I phoned. What else can I do?'

'Go and see the man in charge. *Convince* him.'

'Of course, but it will carry more weight if you come too.'

That caused Jean to think. The pause was enough for Pam Mortimer.

'I'm truly sorry.'

Jean relented but said sharply,

'Very well. I'll come straight away.'

★   ★   ★

O'Hara looked around Seigle's offices, at his people dusting for prints, and decided he was in the way. Outside in the tunnel he looked up and down its length. Since it turned at both ends there was no daylight — no sense of what time of day it was, only the dull fluorescent light.

Later Rhew found his 'Chief' in the computer section, staring thoughtfully at a screen.

'Sir, two doctors want to see you — that psychiatrist, Doctor Mortimer, and Doctor Hacker.'

Tom O'Hara looked up at him, preoccupied for a moment.

'What about?'

His sergeant shrugged.

'I'm guessing it must be about our main suspect, Major Larsson.'

O'Hara shook his head. 'What's the matter with this place — have they all got guilty secrets? O.K. Bring 'em here.'

After Rhew had gone, O'Hara turned back to the computer, pressed for a printout of the details on the screen. The machine began spewing out paper. He took the bit he wanted and ambled to his desk in an area marked off by filing cabinets.

He was sitting studying it when Sergeant Rhew showed in the two doctors.

It was the dark haired one who spoke first.

'Major Larsson, the patient in my care. He can't be your man.'

O'Hara steepled his hands on the desk, clicked his teeth.

'Well that's odd, after all it was you who initially warned us to the possibility of Larsson being involved?'

The red haired one leaned forward onto the desk, and said fiercely,

'I know Major Larsson *personally*. He's had some terrible experiences in Afghanistan, but he's not violent.'

O'Hara's voice was sarcastic.

'Perhaps you should try to tell that to the three men who needed hospital treatment after his attentions.'

'That was different.'

The detective raised an eyebrow.

'Really?' The sarcasm was barely veiled.

Colour came to Jean Hacker's face.

'Yes. It was a case of men fighting — they were escorting him, like a prisoner. It triggered something. He's a trained soldier, but that's not the same as attacking women.'

'That's correct.' Pam Mortimer sounded confident. 'There has never been any suggestion of sexually motivated violence.'

Tom O'Hara didn't immediately reply, but lifted up the computer sheet, frowning, rubbing his cheek with a knuckle.

'I have to say to you that I'm not totally convinced.'

Jean snapped.

'What do you mean?'

He picked up his discarded pipe and tapped with its stem at the printout.

'Major Larsson's wife was murdered.'

Jean protested.

'He told me about that.'

O'Hara continued to look at the flimsy sheet of paper before him, finally murmuring,

'The police never closed the file: he remains a suspect.'

The effect was like a cold hand closing around her heart.

When they left, they went to the medical school cafeteria, conscious of the hushed atmosphere. The police seemed to be everywhere.

After queuing at the self-service counter they went to a table in the corner.

Pam Mortimer pulled off her jacket.

'Phew, it's getting very hot.'

Jean raising her cup to her lips, elbows on the table, nodded.

'That's good. James is out there somewhere.'

With her coat on the back of her chair Pam picked up her own coffee.

'I didn't say anything in there — obviously, but . . .'

Jean put her head on one side.

'But what?'

Pam Mortimer swallowed.

'Please don't jump down my throat — I just wondered if you've been hiding him?'

Jean looked at her, saw that she was genuine.

'No.'

Pam stretched out a hand, squeezed Jean's forearm.

'Cheer up, he'll turn up. That man is a survivor. When you consider what he's been through.'

Jean blinked back the tears.

What she really couldn't say or tell anyone, was that she was worried that James Larsson had gone away for *good*.

★ ★ ★

Disorientated, Annabel with her arms still outstretched, seemed to be floating through space and time, like some star child in the blackness of her universe — a dead universe.

Suddenly she realized that there was something else, some presence near her.

She was not alone.

It wasn't long afterwards that Annabel started to scream.

23

'My God, that's wonderful news.'

At her husband's voice, Thelma O'Hara looked up from her knitting. The TV had been turned down low in order that he could hear the call he had received on the home telephone. As Tom O'Hara listened he put his hand over the mouth piece and spoke to her.

'The girl — Mary — she's O.K. She ran away, back home. Pressure was too much for her.'

Mrs O'Hara dropped her knitting onto her lap.

'Oh that's marvellous.'

He took his hand away from the telephone, barked into it.

'Right. Let her have a good night's sleep. I shall want to see her tomorrow.'

He listened, then said,

'Good. Well, it seems that Dr Seigle might be telling the truth.'

Another pause then.

'Very well, thank you, goodnight.'

He clicked off the phone.

His wife set her needles and wool aside and stood.

'There, I'll make a cup of tea. I knew there must be some good news soon. I couldn't believe *two* girls in quick succession.'

Tom O'Hara got up.

'Thank you my dear, but I need something stronger.'

He went to a side-table, and twisted the top off a bottle. He poured a generous whiskey. Thelma O'Hara paused in the doorway, then came back.

'I'll have one too.'

They clicked glasses.

Tom O'Hara smacked his lips at the first fiery taste of the liquid.

'So, if Dr Seigle is telling the truth, and Larsson is not likely to do something like this, that leaves us George Nieminen.'

He took another mouthful of scotch.

'Let's hope we get him soon — and Annabel is alive.'

But that, he conceded mentally, looked increasingly unlikely.

★　★　★

The technician in charge of the student programme was working late, preparing for the forthcoming exams, setting up specimens and sections in the small laboratory not far from Seigle's room.

He was on the point of finishing when there was a crash from the next room — the main dissecting hall.

He opened the door, reaching for the light switch. Nothing happened for a second, then there was a flash of light, followed by a steady glow from the nearest fluorescent tube, with a following pattern of others that came on until the whole large room was bright with light.

The technician's eyes traversed the rows of white-shrouded bodies.

All seemed in order. He took a nervous step or two further into the cold room, was embarrassed and humiliated to hear his voice so tight and high as he called out,

'Who's there?'

His main concern were the students from the Art Faculty, who were always pestering him to be allowed access to the dissecting hall so that they could sketch exposed muscles — the underlying form of the human shape, as they had in Renaissance Italy.

He'd once found four of them sitting around a cadaver, sketching away like mad.

He advanced further into the room, stopped and looked around.

There was no sign of anyone. But he saw the cause of the noise. A 'bit' bucket was on its side. His gaze lifted. One of the swing doors was still moving gently back and forth.

He strode across, pulled it open and looked out into the corridor. The nearest strip was out, so the only light came from around the corner.

But he could see it was empty — except for a linen trolley.

He turned back into the dissecting room, and took himself to task for not locking the swing doors earlier. His side laboratory had a separate entrance, so there was no need to have left it unsecured.

He got out his keys, locked it and left, shutting off the lighting.

In the returned darkness of the dissecting room nearly sixty pairs of eyes remained fixed, staring unseeing at the white shrouds above them.

Except one pair.

The pupils dilated to allow in as much of the faint light as possible.

Beside them, the rigid dead eyes of another body remained unchanging, reflecting the faint image of the hooded figure who reared up from its ice-cold embrace.

★ ★ ★

That evening Jean waited for a ring on the door that never came. It was as if he had disappeared off the face of the earth. She changed for bed — came back down to the living room and sat in the window, looking out at the drive illuminated by the porch light, hoping to see him appear as if from nowhere. Once she thought she saw a shape detach itself from the darkness of a tree and move to another. She waited for it to happen again; she stared so much that she began to see shapes like men everywhere, an army of phantoms moving through the trees.

It began to rain, at first just the odd spot hitting a leaf, making it twitch, and then the silvery streaks caught in the porch light, merged into a torrent.

Jean's face, reflected in the glass was suddenly full of tears, streaming down her cheeks.

It wasn't entirely an illusion.

Her eyes were moist, and a single diamond-bright drop wound its tortuous way to the corner of her mouth.

She leaned her hot forehead against the cold glass, whispered,

'James — where are you?'

From outside her face was now distorted by the deluge streaming down the window.

She was still like that when the phone rang.

Jean whirled around, stared at it in shock as if it couldn't be happening.

The ring came again.

She reached the table, swept it up.

'James?'

There was no reply.

'James?'

She could hear breathing.

'James, it's all right — I'm alone.'

Still no response.

Jean frowned, felt irritation.

'Who's there?'

Breathing.

Click. The line went dead. Bleakly she stared at the telephone as if in some way it would give up its secret. She punched in recall. The number was withheld.

Who the devil had called her?

The 'who' was unnecessary.

It had been the devil.

24

Night turned into day, a day where no rain fell, but the trees and bushes were motionless in the saturated air beginning to heat in the rising sun. O'Hara looked out of the car window as he was driven to the hospital. The newsboards outside the shops carried headlines on the continuing terror.

He thought of Mary — he was due to see her later. She had waited for Seigle, had heard a peculiar shuffling sound. When it had gone she had run for the only one place she knew she would be safe.

Home.

Whatever else the girl had been up to, however sophisticated and technically trained she was, she had become a terrified child, and had fled back to Ma and Pa.

Thank God she had.

Because Tom O'Hara was by no means certain she would be alive now if she hadn't.

The car swept past the saluting police officer on the gate and reached the side entrance of the Medical School.

He stepped out, looked up at the Gothic

Victorian towers of the old building. It was unfortunately, the right setting for horror.

★　★　★

Charles Seigle and Mary were interviewed separately, Seigle for the second time, and then together. Seigle was adamant. He'd not in any way contacted Annabel, and Mary for her part had to admit that her friend had only spoken of going to see somebody about her state aid. The admin. office knew of no such problem.

When they'd gone O'Hara sat with a cup of coffee and cookies, shared with Rhew. 'What do you think, sir?'

His boss shrugged, dipped his shortcake in the brown liquid.

'They were definitely having a *ménage à trios* — but why would Seigle want to harm her?'

'Maybe she was going to blackmail him, sir.'

'And Marjorie Gooding?'

Rhew faltered, 'A coincidence?'

O'Hara lapsed into silence, broken only by the plopping sound as a bit of his cookie dropped into the coffee.

He finally spoke.

'Never completely rule out coincidence. In

real life it happens a lot.'

Rhew waited, realizing the boss was thinking.

O'Hara rubbed his jaw. Finally he said,

'I want you to feed into the computer the career movements of all the staff of this medical school and hospital. Have it cross-checked with any serious offences in the vicinity of where they were working — go back say ten years. Use the FBI database.'

Rhew jotted it down.

'That's a hell of a lot of people, sir. It will take time.'

'Do it. Start with Seigle — oh, and shove in Major Larsson's details as far as we know them.'

Rhew looked up from his pad.

'How would Larsson be able to lure a student, sir? Attacking at random is one thing, that lets him off surely?'

O'Hara snapped.

'Does it? Not in my book. He's a trained observer, and has been hanging around the hospital. He's resourceful, cunning and dangerous — that's enough for me. He's here somewhere, I'll bet my pension on it. We know the murderer has some place where he tortured Annabel — maybe it's the same place he's holed up.'

* ★ ★

For the next three days they turned the hospital upside down, combed the grounds, descended into drains.

Nothing.

And for those three days and three nights Jean did her best to believe in James Larsson. Every night when she returned to the house she expected to see him, waiting, standing in the drive.

Or in the kitchen — making a cup of coffee, turning, smiling.

But she was always disappointed.

Charles Seigle came and sat opposite her in the cafeteria. He looked unwell and had lost his overbearing manner.

'Jean, have you forgotten about tonight?'

She stared blankly back at him as he stirred his coffee, and continued uneasily.

'I can understand if you don't want to associate with me after what's happened.'

It dawned on her then. It was the Opera Gala Night. What with everything that had gone on, she'd completely forgotten.

But now she was brought up with a start. And it did seem that James Larsson had deserted her.

What other explanation was there? The thought of the aria from Madam Butterfly

240

was more appealing than ever. She felt she too, was waiting in vain for her lover.

She nodded, felt the ache in her throat as she said,

'Of course I'm coming.'

His hand came out, covered hers on the table before she realized what was happening.

'Thank you. I appreciate it. I'll pick you up at 6.30 as arranged.'

Jean was going to make an excuse — find her own way there. Then she remembered that he had said Felicity and Donald Parsons were to be with him.

'O.K., I'll be ready.'

'I'll never forget you for this Jean — *never* — I'll pay you back somehow.'

As she walked away the lump in her throat grew. Jean would have loved to have been going with James.

But he seemed to have rejected her. What other explanation was there?

★   ★   ★

'So there you are.'

Steven confronted her in the Emergency Room. Jean raised an eyebrow at the sharpness of his voice.

'What can I do for you?'

'I'll tell you what you can do — give me a

key to the door of my house.'

His voice carried over the reception area. She looked around, embarrassed.

'For God's sake keep your voice down.'

'Why the hell should I? You changed the lock so now give me the key.'

He jabbed his hand out. It actually touched her, making her step back to keep her balance. The women clerks behind the counter looked up anxiously.

Jean slapped his hand away.

'Our house — and you left it remember — with that bloody skeleton in my shower.'

Jean made to brush past him, but he grabbed her wrist. She twisted her hand away and made off down the corridor.

He called after her.

'Jean — you'll be sorry you've taken this attitude. I have every right to get in the house. If you don't give me the key I shall break in.'

She stopped, turned around, jabbed with a finger.

'Do that, and I'll have you arrested.'

'You can't stop me getting things that belong to me.' He was shouting now.

'Make an appointment,' she snapped. Crimson faced she stalked off.

Steven Hacker made to go after her, then became conscious of all the eyes on them, the rows of waiting patients, the nurses. He ran a hand through his hair, swore under his breath. As he made his way back to the oral surgery department he could think of only one thing.

Jean was a bitch. He would be well rid of her.

★   ★   ★

The dissecting room was bathed in the harsh light of the fluorescent strips — the windowless room was the same, day or night.

But instead of the usual hustle and bustle of chattering students gathered around their work, the room was empty, besides the rows and rows of bodies covered in their white sheets.

Except one.

It lay on a trolley on its own, where all week it had been worked on by John Salter a new staff member of the anatomy department in preparation for the exams. He had dissected several sites: in the head and neck, upper forearm, and brachial plexus and abdomen.

Salter uncovered the cadaver, checked his work was still clear, and then turned his attention to the list of students on his clipboard who were taking the exam. It was going to be a long session, but at least he was going to be relieved at one o'clock.

He nodded at the porter on the door, his voice echoing in the cold room as he called out,

'Right, let's be having the first one.'

The man opened the door.

'Number one, please.'

A youth with glasses came in. Salter smiled at him. It wasn't that long ago that he too had known what it was like to have exam nerves — especially in a practical one, where you could cover a lot of ground.

'Name?'

'John Faulkner.'

He nodded. 'Right then, John, let's start by seeing what you know about the upper arm.'

It went on like that until one o'clock when the door opened, and instead of a student the tall figure of Dr William Henderson, a senior lecturer in anatomy came in. He stood back until Salter finished interrogating a female student on the abdomen.

'Thank you, Miss Fitzgerald.'

The girl smiled confidently and went off as Henderson joined Salter, not saying anything until the latter had finished writing up his notes.

'How's it going?'

Salter handed him the clipboard.

'Not a bad bunch. Maybe the great American public are going to get lucky for once.'

Henderson settled himself on the vacated stool Salter had been using and glanced over the mark he'd given.

'I see — pretty good. Number sixty-four next. Correct?'

Salter looked over his shoulder.

'Yes. I'm off then — what's the dish of the day?'

Henderson grunted. 'Pasta.'

Salter brightened, 'Oh good. See you later.'

As he passed through the doors, number sixty-four, a sandy haired young man entered in response to the porter's call.

He walked up to Henderson, who checked his name then said,

'Very good, let's start with the seventh cranial nerve.'

The student moved to the table as, still seated, Henderson thrust with his legs and wheeled himself nearer, leaning forward as the youth began his answer.

'Well sir, it arises — '

He got no further. Henderson suddenly gasped and shot to his feet.

In horror he stared down at the face. In the prescribed manner it was cut off by a neat line at the forehead, the skull cap removed to display the convoluted brain glistening

245

yellowly in the overhead lights.

The lidless eyes protruded like bulging marbles in their sockets.

The mouth was grinning with demented evil, the molar teeth at the sides exposed by the absence of cheeks.

But despite everything, Henderson instantly recognized the hideous cybernetic-like head for what it had been — for *who* it had been.

It was the missing maintenance worker George Nieminen.

25

Rhew was waiting by the double doors of the dissecting room when O'Hara arrived from City Hall where he had been briefing the mayor.

'The body's in here, sir, with all the others.'

They walked up the aisle, O'Hara looking around at the rows of covered corpses, then finally, under a pool of stronger light, at the reds, blues and yellows that were the mortal remains of George Nieminen.

'Jesus, this is about the most macabre thing I've ever seen.'

Rhew, who had a cold coming, sniffed, and immediately regretted it as the smell of preserving fluid suddenly impinged on his dulled olfactory organ.

'It proves one thing though, doesn't it, sir?'

Tom O'Hara raised a quizzical eyebrow.

'What's that?'

'He can't be the killer.'

Still looking down with horrified fascination at the excruciatingly dismembered Nieminen, O'Hara muttered,

'Maybe he was. Perhaps he saw the killer and tried blackmail.'

Rhew shook his head.

'Not from what they've told me, sir' — he nodded at the doctors standing around in clusters.

'Annabel's disappearance was *after* Nieminen's death and he may have died even before Marjorie Gooding.'

A white-looking Salter interrupted.

'That's right, Superintendent. I carried out the dissection, the body was on the trolley. I thought it had been brought from the storeroom. I've been working on it for over a week. I never knew Nieminen,' he added unnecessarily.

Henderson joined them.

'I've checked the storeroom. There is one specimen too many, so he must have been substituted.'

O'Hara shuddered. He'd seen the refrigerated room where the bodies hung in plastic bags in rows — like a meat packing freezer room.

He waived a hand at the remains.

'I need to know how, and when he was killed — and quick.'

The two doctors looked at each other.

'That's a forensic pathologist's job and it might prove impossible.'

Without another word O'Hara walked away, Rhew caught him up.

'You all right, sir?'

O'Hara snapped. 'Never felt better. What the hell am I to make of this mess?'

He had suddenly felt his age. What a way to end his career.

Rhew glanced uneasily at his boss as he opened the door for him.

'Well, sir, there is a precedent. At Gainesville in Florida, at the university there, four women and a man were brutally killed in just two days. They never . . . '

O'Hara took out the empty pipe he'd just put in his mouth, gave his sergeant an incredulous look.

'Where the hell did you dig that up from?'

John Rhew faltered.

'I googled hospital homicides, sir.'

O'Hara shook his head in disbelief.

'And what else did this worthy source have to offer?'

Rhew wasn't sure whether his boss was being serious or not; his voice had a sarcastic edge.

'It says the more organized killers are less mad than bad, whereas the impulsive ones tend to be suffering from mental illness.'

O'Hara rolled his eyes upwards.

They reached the stairs to the Medical School lobby.

'Anything else?'

'They have fantasies about destruction when young and these become intertwined with sexuality as they get older. They find listening to their victim's pleas for mercy more thrilling than the actual murder or sex.'

O'Hara stopped dead in his tracks, turned and looked Rhew in the eye.

'By God boy, I hope you realize what you've just said.'

Rhew looked after him suddenly feeling sick.

★ ★ ★

The last piece of the gala evening was the Recondita Armonia from *Tosca*.

The tears welled up in Jean's eyes as Puccini's tumultuous soaring music opened her heart, baring it as surely as a surgeon's knife.

Charles Seigle had noticed the effect, had seen her dabbing at her eyes. With the group at the restaurant afterwards Jean ate only lightly, suddenly wanting to go home.

She whispered to Seigle.

'Don't worry, I'll get a cab.'

He pushed his chair back.

'I feel bushed as well.'

At any other time she would have tactfully declined, but the Parsons looked set for a protracted stay.

She protested again, but he continued to insist.

'Well, if you're sure . . . ?'

'Quite. Give me a few moments.'

Jean made her farewells moving around the company.

'It's been a lovely evening — thank you for including me.'

They were good people. She hugged them in turn. No conscious thought had gone through her mind, but as she took leave of them it was as if for the last time.

Perhaps it was.

Jean realized with surprise that the thought must have been growing inside her, at first unknowingly, symptomless, like a malignant tumour until its hold was secure, and it could metastasize. The music of Puccini had done that.

Now it had moved from her heart to her mind and the desire to finish it all claimed her.

Suicide beckoned.

If James Larsson had rejected her as well, then really there was no point in going on: she couldn't face life anymore.

'You enjoyed that didn't you?'

They were in his car. She nodded in the darkness, lit in bursts of half-light from the passing street lamps.

'Yes, very much.'

He smiled. 'I could see that.'

Jean suddenly realized that he had been drinking more than she had been aware of. She gazed fixedly out of the window at the passing sidewalk, resigned for the expected pass.

But without warning Charles Seigle leaned forward, switched on the radio. Soft music filtered into the interior and he seemed to become preoccupied.

When they finally swung into her drive the headlights reflected back from the dead dark windows of the house.

There were no signs of life.

No sign of James.

Not that she had expected it.

Even old Seigle, with his reputation, was good to have there just then.

With the latest awful news of the fate of the maintenance engineer, she — like all the hospital staff — was becoming increasingly edgy.

She smiled inwardly at the irony — to be fearful of a death which she was contemplating anyway.

But suicide was one thing: torture and murder at the hands of a madman quite another.

Against all her better judgements, she had

a sudden fear that Charles Seigle would just leave her at the front door.

'You'll come in for coffee?'

The courtesy light flooded the interior of the car.

Seigle smiled. 'Of course. If that's what you want.'

'It will have to be a quickie though, got to be up early tomorrow.'

Inside the pitch-black hall her hand found the light switch. It was good to have company. She resolved to go upstairs and into all the rooms before he left.

Jean pushed open the living-room door and flicked on the light, indicating the TV and the music centre.

'Make yourself at home for a minute.'

With the kettle on she ran upstairs, turning on lights and looking into all the rooms.

In Steven's she was turning away, hand on the switch, when her eyes fell on the large, old fashioned closet. She hesitated, cross with herself for being childish, but knew it was no good — there was no way she could go into her bedroom — and *sleep* — without first looking into its interior. Also, there might be another of Steven's jolly little 'japes' waiting for her.

Her irritation overflowed. Flinging the door open she fisted the hanging clothes inside.

253

Nowhere did she touch anything solid — like a man's body.

She left her bedroom to the last. It was empty. Jean turned off the light and ran lightly downstairs. Back in the kitchen she made coffee, loaded it onto a tray and carried it into the living room.

'There we are . . . '

The room was empty.

She stopped dead in her tracks.

'Charles?'

Her voice almost failed her. Jean set the tray down.

'Charles, where are you?'

She opened the door to the dining-room and looked in.

Empty.

Tense, Jean closed the door and swung around — straight into his arms. Her scream gurgled into silence as Seigle held on to her.

'What's going on?'

She took her hand that had fled instinctively to her throat and used it to discreetly free herself from his embrace.

'Where were you?'

He swayed a little.

'I've been to the bathroom. You OK.?'

Relieved, she walked to the tray, smoothing down her dress.

'It's just, well I'm a little on edge on my

own in this big house, what with all this dreadful business at the hospital. I'm going to move you know.'

He raised a dark eyebrow as she gave him his coffee.

'When?'

'As soon as possible.'

Jean sat down on the sofa, aware of his staring at her legs. She pulled at her hem as they drank and talked about the evening's performances until quite unexpectedly he suddenly set his cup down on the table and stood up.

'Jean, I can't thank you enough for the support you've shown me tonight.'

She shrugged. 'It was nothing.'

She led the way to the hall door, opened it.

He followed, stood closer than manners dictated.

'Goodnight, Charles.'

She went up onto her toes to give him a peck on his cheek, just as he turned his face towards her.

His lips were wet, cold, and to her disgust she felt his tongue pushing into the gap between her partly open teeth.

'Thanks.'

With that he stepped outside. Without waiting for him to get in his car, she quickly closed the door, sagged back against it, listening as he started the engine and drove off.

In the silence she began to shake. She hurried to the bathroom and found a mouthwash. Its biting, antiseptic taste scoured and cleaned the inside of her violated mouth.

★   ★   ★

James Larsson awoke from a deep sleep to see directly over him a full moon riding high in the heavens, wisps of fleecy cloud racing into the blue penumbra, moving on past, to be swallowed up again in the velvet starlit blackness. The outline of the ferns above his face formed a pattern like a delicate celestial lace. He lay without moving, conscious of the smell near him — pungent, characteristic, its source no more than a couple of feet away. When he silently reared up, moving from the waist only, soil falling aside like a corpse rising from burial, the skunk turned tail and fled, while the viper that had been coiled near his head, slithered silently away into the undergrowth.

Larsson's head slowly rotated, scanning, seeming almost mechanical, then tilted back until the moon caught his eyes. They glowed, dull, yellow, a hunter-killer in the night black jungle of his mind.

Was he awake, whatever that meant. Or was this the start of another dream — another nightmare? Were the moon, the earth, the fine throngs of ferns, the towering gothic columns of the half-seen trees real — or in his imagination?

And did it even matter? What was reality? Was it what he saw, or what he *thought* he saw?

Perhaps even his mind was its own reality: what it believed was paramount, nothing else mattered.

And what it believed in was revenge.

Like a black wraith he rose higher, growing out of the very earth itself.

* * *

Jean Hacker lay with the same moonlight falling onto her pillow. In sleep, her face caught in its soft glow and was troubled, restless, as if some primitive part of her was aware of the powerful life force that was now perilously close to her, moving to envelope her in its black coils, to take her life, to take her soul into its possession.

And then destroy her.

26

The morning was still and misty, the dew on the neat grass leading down to the greenhouse glistened in the sunshine like millions of diamonds.

Tom O'Hara returned to the house, decided not to take his waterproofs despite his wife's protest that the weather forecast was for severe thunderstorms later that day, kissed her goodbye and marched out to his waiting car. He hoped to be home by the time the rough weather arrived.

When he was comfortably ensconced in the back seat the driver handed him a pile of newspapers.

'You ordered these, sir?'

O'Hara grunted. He knew he wasn't going to like what he was about to read, but he wanted to be fully conversant with the media's reaction in case the mayor called . . .

And he wasn't disappointed as he looked down with distaste at the first tabloid notorious for its past lack of sensitivity. Its banner headline read,

Gutted.

The words appeared above a picture of

Nieminen's body bag being removed down the steps of the Medical School.

But he had to admit a begrudging respect for the copy writer's brevity.

It was to the point.

But his thoughts were for Annabel. By now he had privately given up all hope of finding her alive.

And with this maniac, when she did show, where would it be? No dreadful little grave half scooped out of earth and covered with leaves — that was not his style if Nieminen's disposal was anything to go by.

It was as if he had to dump his victims' bodies right under the noses of the authorities.

A challenge? Come and get me if you can. Or . . .

O'Hara took the pipe out of his mouth as he tried to get his brain around the idea that had just hit him.

Not so much come and get me as —

You *can't* get me, but I can get you — *anytime*.

Fear. He was doing it to deliberately spread fear.

And that was the philosophy of one group of men; men trained to kill, to create destruction — to send ahead of themselves an aura of terror before they even struck.

And James Larsson was a member of that group. A *flawed* member.

The car turned into the hospital and drove up to the Medical School past a crowd gathered outside.

Inside there was a scene of urgent police activity. They looked at each other, Rhew grabbing the arm of a passing officer.

'What's happened?'

The man spoke with a strong southern accent.

'We're getting reports of a woman's body, sir.'

O'Hara's heart turned to stone.

'Where?'

'I believe they're taking it out of the river about now.'

He grimaced.

'Keep me posted.'

But somehow he didn't think it would be Annabel, unless the killer was panicking.

Panic?

Not their man. He wouldn't know the meaning of the word.

★　★　★

All day the police presence was high profile. Teams of officers patrolled in two's along the corridors.

It was, O'Hara knew, in part a reaction to the media's attention, which had increased public fear: they had to be seen to be doing something.

But he remembered an old-timer complaining that his investigation of a serial rapist had been hampered by the need to have more men patrolling than were actually on the detection side for the same reason. And if his hunch was right, their maniac would strike again — and soon. Just like Rhew's Gainsville episode. He had the feeling they were all sitting on top of a volcano — waiting for it to erupt.

At eleven o'clock the computer displayed a screen of information that sent him reaching for the phone to make an appointment.

He was shown into Pam Mortimer's office. She stood up to greet him.

'Do take a seat.'

'Thank you.'

Her finely shaped left eyebrow raised quizzically.

'Now, what's this about — as if I can't guess?'

O'Hara nodded, lips set firmly.

'Larsson, he's not as safe as you make out.'

'Oh.'

Did he detect a certain knowingness in her look as she continued.

'I stick by my assessment. The man was brought in with acute post-stress problems — not sexual ones.'

O'Hara looked steadily back at her as he tossed onto the desk the printed-off information that had arrived from the Pentagon.

'Better take a look at these, *Doctor*.'

She drew them slowly to her, glancing up at him before reading them, becoming more absorbed and utterly silent. When she finally looked up it was to find him still staring intently at her.

He nodded. 'Yes. He was present, as a very young soldier, at the aftermath of the rape and murder of several women in Iraq.'

'This,' she faltered, 'makes terrible reading — especially for a psychiatrist.'

O'Hara shifted uneasily in his chair.

'It's terrible reading for a policeman, Doctor. Why especially for you?'

She tapped a finger on the printed-off sheets.

'From previous reports he was subjected to prolonged sleep deprivation. It's scrambled his mind.'

The policeman grunted.

'Are you telling me now he is some sort of walking zombie?'

Pam Mortimer drew in her breath.

'Yes, that's exactly what I'm getting at.

People who have been made to stay awake for days — weeks — well, they can go into a dream-like state and yet they appear awake to everyone around them. But they can live in their dream — perceive events, people, interpret them differently. And this was undoubtedly a traumatic moment for a young man and will have left its scar.'

Tom O'Hara thought for a moment before finding her eyes again.

'And what, Doctor, is the position if he is in a nightmare?'

★　★　★

Jean came home at six, exhausted from a hard, difficult day in a very disrupted department.

The evening was very humid, and across the city skyline as her car had climbed the hill she had seen a yellowish haze hanging over the rooftops.

The silence in the house was oppressive. Again she had been disappointed, had this time cried as she had found no James waiting for her. He had completely vanished.

Jean poured a good measure of gin into a tumbler, added ice, her fumbling hands sending some cubes bouncing across the floor. She left them, adding tonic from a large

263

plastic bottle and then disconsolately moved into the living room.

She put on a CD. As the music crashed out, enveloping her in a storm of violins and booming timpani, she went to the french windows, held her feverish head against the cold glass.

Would she ever see him again? Was he all right, perhaps he was lying injured somewhere?

She was well aware that her body ached not with the wild erotic music of a man called Wagner. It was in turmoil for another man, an urge so fundamental that it seemed to sweep through her civilized soul like a forest fire. Doctor Jean Hacker knew without doubt that she would defy the law, would break it, would totally disregard it in the maelstrom of alien urges destroying the woman she had been.

And she didn't care. Only one thing mattered. That he should come to her.

And if he didn't, she would finish it all.

The bushes at the bottom of the garden suddenly quivered, a bird flew away.

For the first time she noticed the angry blue-black clouds towering in the sky, evoking in her, with the help of the music, childhood fantasies — that the clouds were mountains with, if you stared hard enough, dark, forbidding castles.

The clouds reached the house, seemed to be closing over her like a giant fist. A deep, faraway rumble rattled a window pane.

With the approaching storm came once again the feeling of isolation. Seconds later the rain came.

It was a storm that was to last on and off for most of the night, and when it finally finished it would take with it the torment of Jean Hacker.

For ever.

The telephone rang at six fifteen. Momentarily Jean stared at it, then nearly knocked it to the floor in her haste.

'Hello?'

'Are you alone?'

It was *him*. Emotion made it difficult for her to speak.

'Yes.'

There was a pause which she filled with a panic-stricken.

'Hello, are you still there?'

To her relief Larsson's voice came again.

'Yes. Jean — can I come to you — now?'

It was difficult to get her breath.

'Of course.'

'You know they are looking for me?'

'I don't care. Where are you, I'll bring the car.'

'No'. His voice was harsher. He relented.

'I'll come in after dark. Leave the doors unlocked, and the windows. Keep all the lights out — *understand?*'

'Yes.'

The line went dead. No tender sentiments. No thank yous. She lowered the receiver. It didn't matter. He was in trouble — and he was coming to her. All of a sudden she could understand the actions of infatuated women.

Now the madness was on her, destroying everything she had believed herself to be. Soon she would be sheltering a man wanted by the police — a man they considered to be highly dangerous, perhaps . . . a killer?

Even as she gulped her drink, unknown to her the telephone landline lost its current, the blue instrument a useless piece of coloured plastic.

And her cell phone, which she had been searching for since she had been unable to find it in her locker, lay shattered in the rain.

She was isolated from the outside world.

27

The ER was at its quietest at nine o'clock in the evening, before the casualties of the trade in alcohol arrived and kept the staff busy until 3 a.m.

In the waiting area several people sat on the rows of padded benches, others stood around the coffee dispensing machine, while two more were checking in at reception. A member of the hospital's own private security staff stood talking to two policemen at the door, their dark blue uniforms standing out against the pastel shaded room and its drably clothed people.

Cleaners mopped the floor in between a roped off section, with a sign on a mobile post that read 'Danger: Wet Floor'. Others moved down the long corridor between cubicles, emptying the bins and wiping down cupboards and walls with disinfectant.

In cubicle fourteen, an Afro-American lady of ample girth confronted a mess. The waste-bin was overflowing with disposable wrappings and stained dressings, but it was the examination couch that took her attention. On it was a great pile of used linen, some of it bloodstained.

She clicked her tongue, grumbled out loud to herself.

'This is disgraceful. What are the nurses thinking of leaving this stuff like that?'

Out of routine she disposed of the waste bin first, dumping the rubbish and its white bag into the lined metal container of her trolley, then replacing it with a fresh one. She wiped her disinfected rag on several cupboards, then got out her mop for the floor, before remembering the examination couch and its pile. Still tutting she went over and spread her arms out, intending to sweep up the pile in one go.

Except her hands touched something solid.

Human flesh.

Delicately she lifted the top sheet to get a view of what she dreaded — the damned nurses should have told her they had left a body in here awaiting collection instead of letting her get into this position.

As soon as she saw what it was, she knew that the nurses didn't know about this one.

This had been a young woman.

And it had had terrible things done to it — like the tales she had heard of voodoo back home — in the old folks' country.

Her eyes went wide, the whites in dramatic contrast to her dark brown skin.

It was some seconds before her screams had the police and security men, doctors, nurses and even some of the patients joining in the rush to get to cubicle fourteen.

But they were all too late for Annabel.

★   ★   ★

The silence in the dark house was broken by a clock chiming in the dining-room. Jean sat in the kitchen, facing the back door. Time no longer had any meaning for her.

The storm had come and gone — for now — leaving only a distant, uneasy rumbling that presaged more rain and thunder.

The air in the room was heavy. In the window a spider remained utterly motionless, its delicate web caught in the blue flickering of the far-off lightning.

But then something happened. It came in the opposite direction, from the door into the hall. She had been waiting for so long that she 'felt' the movement rather than heard a sound — almost as if she had perceived it by a sense that had no name, that had developed in the long silent hours of heightened self-awareness.

Slowly she stood up, waited, aware of movement coming nearer, finally stopping just on the other side of the door.

Seconds passed.

The door stayed shut. Her night-accustomed eyes never left the handle.

'James.' Her voice was a whisper.

'Is that you?'

Silence.

Jean could wait no longer. Tense with suppressed excitement she flung the door open and stepped into the dark hall . . .

It was empty.

'James?' This time her voice faltered. She advanced further, stood beside the bannister suddenly conscious that the outside porch light was on, sending bars of red and green along one wall as the rays passed through the stained glass side windows.

Disappointed, she called again.

'Hello? I'm here.'

There was no reply.

The porch light puzzled her. She'd more than followed his instructions, not even putting on the bedroom light. But then it had been daylight — perhaps it had been on all day and that's why she hadn't noticed it.

She swung open the front door, looked out. There was no sign of anyone. Giant moths from the woods fluttered in the poor light, reminding her in their jerking flight of bats. It wasn't raining, but the humidity was high, and a yellow mist drifted around the trees.

The earth and bushes seemed to be exuding hot moist gasses devoid of oxygen. She turned back as another rumble broke from the uneasy heavens, and closed the door.

The porch light went out, leaving the house in darkness. Seconds passed before a ripple of light ran across the sky, picking out the towering clouds of another storm.

★ ★ ★

Detective O'Hara's car pulled up at the ER entrance, its blue flashing light almost lost in the torrential cloud burst.

He said to Sergeant Rhew as the latter put his hand on the car door to get out,

'Stay where you are, boy, a few minutes won't make any difference to the poor lass.'

Under his breath he swore at the struggling faces of the reporters pressed to rain lashed car windows. The press corp was getting bigger by the hour with TV network vans, with their roof mounted dishes, lining the forecourt.

The chilling news had reached O'Hara as he had been taking a cold shower.

Despite the heat and humidity he had actually shivered.

He looked at the baying mob outside, at the strong lights now coming on for the video cameras, and the flashes for the still shots.

What a circus.

And over it all the rain lashed down. The tears of the Gods.

When he finally got in he found the corridor blocked with people — he couldn't reach the cubicle doorway. Something snapped. Even Rhew jumped as his normally laconic boss suddenly roared out.

'Get this circus — OUT. Everybody *OUT*. This is a crime scene goddamit.'

Galvanized into action the uniformed officers present ushered everybody away. It took a minute before Tom O'Hara found himself looking down at the broken doll that had been Annabel, and the terrible things that had been done to her. He turned away. Somehow he felt he had failed her — that she had depended upon him and he had let her down. And the killer had dumped her — arrogantly — right in the busiest department. He felt this latest discovery slapped his face: it was personal now.

Back in the reception area he nodded to the forensic team.

'Right — she's all yours.'

Then he saw the elderly couple standing clutching each other for support in the main doorway, blue lights flashing outside behind them. Their clothes were wringing wet. But it was their faces that instantly announced *who* they were. He swore under his breath that this had been allowed to happen, then he swallowed and made his way towards Annabel's parents.

★   ★   ★

Jean never heard a thing. She returned to the kitchen, and quickly poured a glass of wine, by the light from the open fridge door, then made her way in the darkness to the living-room. She settled into her favourite armchair facing the door to the hall.

She'd just taken a sip of her drink when she suddenly froze.

There was somebody in the room. She could see nothing, hear nothing, but . . .

'Hello Jean.'

His voice was only a whisper.

'James?'

He moved, and for the first time she saw him sitting in a winged chair in the corner. The dark shape leaned forward, and the vague light from the window fell on his face. She could see the scar.

She found her voice: it trembled.

'How long have you been there?'

'Some time.'

It hurt. 'Don't you trust me?'

He whispered — 'With my life.'

Jean went to him, sinking to her knees as his arms encircled her.

They held on to each other, not speaking. It was minutes before Jean kissed him, long and tenderly. When she sat back on her heels, she asked,

'Where have you been? Why didn't you get in touch?'

He reached out and stroked her hair.

'I couldn't — believe me.'

'But where were you?'

He nodded his head in the direction of the forest.

'Out there.'

She frowned.

'What did you live on?'

'Oh little beasties, bigger beasties.'

She got to her feet, face creased in horror.

'You must be hungry?'

He smiled. 'A sandwich would be nice.'

Jean squeezed his hand, then let go.

'I'll make some. Can I put the lights on now?'

'No.' It wasn't said harshly, but there was no arguing. Larsson added softly. 'Draw the curtains then we'll just use one candle.'

She did as she was told. With the candle lit she turned, and faced him again.

It was strange, after all the days and nights

of longing, to see him there in the candlelight, his shadow flickering on the wall behind him.

She paused at the door.

'Promise me you'll never go away again?'

'I promise.'

★ ★ ★

It had been distressing — the worst episode of his professional life. Never before had parents of the victim actually turned up at the scene of the crime while the body was still there — in situ.

Dejected, Tom O'Hara returned to the medical school along the tunnels of the old Victorian building. He was aware of the atmosphere of terror.

In his imagination, helped by the old white tiled walls, he sensed the shadow of Jack the Ripper. What with the nurses going around in groups, as had the prostitutes in the warren of streets that was Whitechapel, the atmosphere of fear that prevailed in gas-lit London all those years ago now stalked this small city of a hospital.

And the killer was taunting him.

O'Hara felt his temper rising. He stopped dead in his tracks, looked back at the door to Seigle's office.

Mary, the student, thought she'd heard *something*, thought she was about to be attacked, but could it be that the killer wasn't coming for her — just that he was hiding nearby — that Annabel had been kept nearby?

He could see in one direction to the stairs to the Medical School.

O'Hara noticed a solid door, smaller than normal, under the arch made by the winding staircase.

He looked from it back to the office and back again. Something drew him to it, like a moth to a flame.

As he walked towards the door he knew the room beyond must have been searched, his orders had been to go into every nook and cranny in the entire complex.

O'Hara reached it, twisted the knob, pushed, expected it to be locked. Despite its heavy appearance it opened easily.

He had to stoop to enter. His nostrils were assailed by a musty smell, and there was no light, only pitch blackness. He saw a switch, a big old Victorian affair on the wall and flicked it down.

In the dull yellow light he could see rows and rows of floor-to-ceiling shelves filled with brown covered documents.

O'Hara wandered further in, stood looking

around, ran a finger along the backs of the folders as he walked down the aisle between bays.

The door closed silently behind him.

He stopped, pulled a folder out. Before he could open it he had to blow off the dust, and a small spider ran to the edge and abseiled to the floor.

It was details of a student at the Medical School forty-odd years ago.

It was depressing to think that the sunlit far-off days of his youth were now also confined to a dark dusty mausoleum like this.

He remembered Annabel's pathetic remains, grunted. At least he had a life to look back on.

It was as quiet as the grave in the archive room, the towering shelves full of reams of paper acted as an effective absorber of what little noise penetrated its bunker-like depth.

Tom O'Hara reached the end and found himself looking at yet another door. This one was arched with a stone surround.

He tried it, but it didn't budge. O'Hara stood back, attempted to figure out where it went, and realized that whatever was there, must be deep under the street.

And then he heard a rustling sound. He froze as he remembered Mary's description, and wished that Rhew was with him.

He turned around slowly, and saw only the

gloomy rows of long forgotten records, of long forgotten lives.

Still the sound persisted, and he felt the faintest of tremors in the floor. Tom O'Hara actually felt the hair on his head prickle. His hand found his holster with its .38 nestling in its embrace.

It took some time before he realized what it was — rain coursing to earth through old pipes as thunderbolts fell to earth above.

He released his grip on the pistol and turned back to the door, tried again. It was solid, wouldn't budge.

O'Hara kicked the bottom of it as he turned away. If he couldn't establish damn quick whether it had been searched or not, he wouldn't hesitate to have it opened with axes if that's what it took.

★ ★ ★

When Jean returned it was to find he had turned on the television, without the sound, the light from its screen flickering on his face as he sat on a sofa.

She set the plate down on the coffee table. 'There you are.'

She turned to look at him when he didn't immediately reply. It was then she realized that he wasn't actually watching anything. It was as if he was asleep with his eyes open. It was spooky.

Even as she reached out some sign of life came into the vacant pupils.

He smiled at her, then looked at the tray. 'Thanks.'

She sat down beside him, watching as he drank and ate. Although ravenous, she could see he was pacing himself.

When he was finished he sat back. Jean moved nearer, was happy when his arm came out around her, settling her against his chest. She could hear the steady thump of his heart, felt the hardness of the muscles of his arm.

For the first time in her life she experienced a sense of belonging, of being cherished and protected.

'Jean,' he murmured.

'Yes?'

'You know very little about me.'

She set her mouth firmly.

'I know enough.'

'Don't you want to know more about my past?'

Her face clouded.

'No. Not ever, unless you feel the need to tell me.'

He smiled.

'Maybe one day.'

This time he *closed* his eyes.

Jean watched him for a while, then remembered that he was wanted by the police.

'James, what's going to happen? What are we going to do?'

Still with his eyes closed he said,

'Let's not worry now. Something will turn up.' But he had noted the 'we'.

It was some time before he said,

'I take it I can stay the night?'

'Need you ask?'

He opened his eyes.

'Are you sure?'

She blushed like an eighteen year old. There could be no doubt at what he meant. Staying the night implied so much more, after all he was a wanted man.

'I'm sure.'

He squeezed her gently, then leaned back pulling her against him.

In seconds he was asleep, leaving her with the blood racing in her body.

Looking at him, Jean stroked his hair gently away from his face, then rested her head on his chest.

Unseeing, uncaring, she idly watched the screen which occasionally burst into white 'snowstorms' of static as another electrical storm moved nearer.

The news came on. A reporter was standing in front of a building at night, his mackintosh streaming with water despite the umbrella in one hand; he held a mike in the other. 'Live' was emblazoned on the top corner of the screen.

The rain was torrential. Suddenly she tensed, recognizing the building behind the reporter as the hospital. She thumbed the remote so that the sound came on low.

' . . . in view of the latest gruesome find coming so closely on the murder of two other members of staff, the police are taking no chances.

'Tonight, the hospital has uniformed men on every floor, and all staff are to be quizzed and warned to take precautions. Heavily armed police are patrolling the grounds.

'This is Martin Cohen for News — '

★   ★   ★

Jean frowned. What gruesome find?

What had happened since she had left work?

She had no time for further thought. Thunder rumbled on and on, suddenly ending with an extra loud detonation that shook the windows.

James Larsson jerked forward, eyes wide and blazing, his hand gripping her throat so tightly that she couldn't breath.

She managed to croak.

'James. Stop.'

A second passed before she saw recognition dawn. He released his grip, shook his head.

'I'm sorry. I thought . . . '

Jean rubbed her neck.

'It's all right. I'm all right.'

She was going to say lots of things, so that he would know that she understood about the past, about Afghanistan, about his wife, about everything. Instead instinct took over. She threw her arms around him.

His mouth closed around hers.

Heart thumping she finally breathed.

'Lets go upstairs.'

He nodded, whispered,

'You go ahead. I'll be up shortly.'

She kissed him once more, and stood up. He was right. She had things to do.

The thunder rumbled again, and the television dimmed before flickering back to normal.

She made for the door.

'I've got candles' — she paused, added softly — 'in the bedroom.'

After she had gone Larsson sat back. It was some time before he became aware of a tinkling — a high-pitched sound like a fluttering Chinese mobile in a breeze.

28

In the bedroom Jean crossed to the window and started to pull the drapes. Sudden vivid lightning lit the view like bright daylight as nature arced its raw power in a jagged darting tongue to earth in the forest.

Through the glass streaming with water she could see the trees swaying wildly in the rain lashed wind as the thunder cracked and rumbled, and finally snapped at her ears in a deafening crump.

She put the small bedside light on while she searched for matches, and lit the ornamental candles attached to her Victorian dressing-table.

She left the sidelight on as she opened the third drawer of an antique chest and took out a black satin nightdress with thin shoulder straps. It was simple, elegant, highly expensive, and very romantic, so different from her normal run-of-the-mill stuff.

For a second her face clouded at the memories it evoked. Jean had bought it in a desperate attempt to entice Steven.

It had proved futile.

Fumbling, she unbuttoned and stepped out

of her skirt, placing it over the back of a chair. Before removing her blouse she unhooked her gold chain, pouring it into her jewel box and snapping the lid shut.

She'd just stepped from the last of her garments when the bedside light dimmed, brightened again and went out.

For a moment, before her eyes grew accustomed to the dark, the candles seemed to burn without light. Their reflection in the mirror looked like the two yellow eyes of a huge cat. With difficulty she felt her way into the nightdress, reaching up to let the smooth soft material slide down over her.

Suddenly a vivid incandescent blue light appeared around the closed drapes, silently bathing her naked extended body in its flickering light.

As soundlessly as it had come the lightning vanished.

Terrified, she waited in the returned darkness.

The noise came first as a hissing crack that hurt her ears, then a tremendous crump and boom of the thunderclap directly overhead, vibrating the floor beneath her feet, setting glass ornaments tinkling.

When it was over she sat down at her dressing-table, the candles now glowing with a warmer light that bathed her face and shoulders in its soft halo.

She looked searchingly at her reflection. Her eyes, still with make-up on, appeared large, mysterious, her lips redder and fuller than she was accustomed to seeing them. The skin of her face and neck was alive with an unusual warmth and texture.

She shook her head, letting the mane of auburn hair swish across her shoulders, realizing nature was playing its part. Her body seemed to be super-sensitive, alive with a fiery intensity as it prepared itself for a ritual that nature had ordained for it since the evolution of mankind.

She began brushing her hair, watching it gleam in the candle-light.

There was no noise. One minute her face was alone in the dancing circle of light in the mirror . . . then quite simply it was not.

Slowly, it just appeared, like something in a child's magic painting book; emerging from the surrounding blackness.

Except it was no child's painting, but a terrible head from the nightmare regions of the human mind.

Two eyes glittered behind the 'V' shaped slits in a woollen hood.

Eyes that burned with a fierce madness.

Eyes that she instantly recognized.

She was paralysed with fear, not just from terror, but the unfairness of life, and the even greater unfairness of death — the terrible death that she knew this thing would inflict upon her.

★　★　★

Detective Tom O'Hara found Rhew with two civilian operatives and a uniformed woman officer gathered around a computer screen.

He drew his sergeant aside.

'There's a locked room — at the back of the old archives room downstairs in the basement. I want confirmation — '

He stopped, chopped his hand in the air.

'No — I want the Hospital Manager to get keys. I want to see in there for myself, now.'

Frowning, Rhew regarded his chief with suspicion.

'What's worrying you, sir?'

O'Hara shrugged.

'Don't know. Just a feeling. But that room would have been perfectly placed . . . for where he . . . '

He didn't have to say more.

'I'll get onto it right away, sir.'

Rhew hurried away. O'Hara turned to the group, and to the leading civilian operative who wanted to talk to him.

'We've had something come up on the FBI records search.'

O'Hara followed her to another terminal. She quickly typed in the code. There was a brief pause and then a heading came up on the screen.

'INCIDENTS OF A SIMILAR NATURE'

In chronological order there followed seven murders, two in Texas; one in Maine, another in New Jersey a fifth in Colorado, and the sixth and seventh in New York.

O'Hara ran his eye along the lines, noting that the forensic details of the savage sexual assaults on Marjorie Gooding and Annabel were almost identical to them all, confirmed by the computer which flashed up on the screen, an eighty per cent similarity assessment. George Nieminen did not fit into the pattern.

The operative said,

'It's a wonder nobody has seen a connection before?'

Tom O'Hara scratched his jaw, touched his finger on the screen.

'Given the timescale, and the widespread geographical sites, perhaps it's not so surprising.'

Moments later Rhew returned and said to O'Hara's back,

'They've promised to have keys here in

fifteen minutes. I can't find out if the room has been searched or not, sir — sir?'

O'Hara stood aside, jerked his head at the screen.

'Take a look at this.'

Rhew stepped forward and began to read.

He was younger than O'Hara, and less disciplined in his ways.

He let his breath out in a whistle.

★   ★   ★

The eyes in the mirror seemed to have a disembodied, separate existence, boring into her, their malevolence alive with an inner fire.

Then another tremendous clap of thunder turned the nightmare back into horrific reality.

Jean Hacker became aware of a shrill, high pitched sound. It went on and on and on as terror closed its icy fingers around her crazed mind. Then she realized what it was:

She was screaming.

Suddenly, uncontrollably, her body jerked upright. Kicking the stool aside she fled to the bedroom door, struggled to open it.

The black inhuman figure made no attempt to follow, turning slowly, like a robot.

It had plenty of time to reach her, but remained motionless.

Finally the door came free and crashed against the wall. Jean reached the top of the stairs, her driving panic forcing her over the edge without concern for the steps.

At the bottom lay the front door, and freedom: freedom from the terrible figure.

Halfway down the stairs she lost her footing and fell, rolling over and over. Everything was sucked into a nightmare vortex of images — walls, pictures, ceiling, the door . . . and the black figure standing on the landing, caught in another flare of flickering blue incandescence.

But this time it started to move, coming down on her.

Terrifyingly fast.

The only sound was her own whimpering, and the grandfather clock, its stately measured beat seemingly enormous in the intense silence between the claps of thunder.

The black cowled figure towered over her and for the first time a rasping hiss emerged from the obscene redness of its mouth.

'You recognize me, don't you Jean?'

She didn't answer, but the masked head nodded — just the once.

'Yes, that's *right.*'

She found strength from somewhere.

'You killed all the others, poor Marjorie, and the girl . . . '

The head lowered to the chest just the once in acknowledgment.

'Yes.' The word was said softly.

She looked again into the awful eyes.

The fire seemed to have gone.

What was left was worse:

Emptiness. She wondered why she hadn't seen it before.

The figure suddenly bent forward, reached for her. Jean jerked away with fear.

The gloved hand hesitated, then gently touched her leg.

'Don't be afraid.'

The head sniggered, a strange, incongruous sound.

'We've got all the rest of your life.'

Then his stiffened hand came from nowhere, struck her at the great nerve plexus at the root of her neck, a chop that dropped her like a felled chicken.

He picked her up, her arms and legs dangling limply, head swinging, auburn hair hanging down from her upturned face, and took her back up the stairs.

The scene was etched in the intense brilliance of a new burst of lightning.

29

Tom O'Hara's guts were churning, and Tom O'Hara never ignored his plumbing. Rhew said,

'New York — that's the date around about when — '

O'Hara was unusually gruff.

'Larsson's wife died, I know.'

A chance date that coincided, in a city where violence was never far below the surface. Not much, but . . .

'Would you like to see the room now, sir?' Rhew held up a huge old key. 'This has just been delivered. The place was searched several days ago.'

'Who searched it?'

'It was on a checklist used by one of the teams drafted in from up-state.'

'Very well, let's go and have a look.'

Tom O'Hara took out his pipe, put his other hand on the computer operator's shoulder.

'While we're away there's something else I'd like you to do.'

Soon her computer was talking to another in the FBI's ViCap automated case matching system, part of the Violent Criminal Apprehension Program at Quantico, Washington DC.

★ ★ ★

The room was a disappointment, small and windowless, with paint peeling from its brick walls, and it was lit from a single shadeless bulb. The floor was stone covered, uneven. The place smelt of damp.

On the floor were stacked dusty-looking cardboard boxes, the end wall was piled high with them.

Who ever had searched the place had pulled some aside and left them scattered.

Disconsolately O'Hara picked his way amongst them, shifting one with his foot, noticed the contents — old exam papers. He picked one out.

It was for Histology.

C.J. Hargreaves. Obtained eighty-four per cent, February Nineteen hundred and ten.

O'Hara grunted. He wondered if C.J. Hargreaves had survived the Great War.

'It's been done over all right by the boys. Nothing here, sir.'

Rhew moved restlessly around the small area.

There was *nothing*. Yet O'Hara was still

292

unhappy. His sergeant went back and stood by the door and waited pointedly. O'Hara let him wait. He pulled another box aside. It was heavy, packed with documents all written in a spidery Victorian hand.

O'Hara finally bowed to the inevitable. He turned back to Rhew and was going to say, 'Very well, I've seen enough.'

Then his eyes fell on the back of the door which had closed gently behind them.

Sergeant Rhew suddenly realized the boss wasn't looking at him. He glanced around, saw only the door then tried to follow O'Hara's line of sight.

He didn't need to be told the implication of what O'Hara was looking at. The fact that it was new, and that there would be no need for it unless you wanted to stop people coming into a room full of old records, while you were inside, was sufficient to send alarm bells ringing.

A *bolt*.

Tom O'Hara came across, looked at it, but did not touch.

'Get the tech boys here — *fast*.'

Rhew almost doubled up to go through the low door.

Left alone O'Hara turned back into the room. A pulse thumped in his temple. Suddenly he knew.

Something in him snapped. The bastard was close, so close. He ran at the end wall covered with boxes, pulling, kicking, throwing them aside — sweating, punching, dragging them down, until he saw it: another door. Despite its age it opened smoothly.

In seconds he was looking at descending stone steps leading into the past from which an overpowering odour of damp and decay flowed out into the present.

And something else.

He'd smelt it once before in his life, in a house where the husband had used a butcher's cleaver on his family — wife, three children, an au pair, then hung himself. Two weeks later O'Hara had forced an entry. He'd never forgotten the smell of old blood, and of rotting putrescent flesh.

Hesitantly, he edged down the steps.

Inside was an absolute blackness.

O'Hara froze, trying to detect the sound of movement, of breathing — of imminent, lethal danger. This time he pulled out his .38.

When a sound came he snarled into the unknown.

'Come on then, you bastard.'

Rhew's head appeared above him.

'You all right, sir?'

O'Hara sagged against the wall, realized his heart was thumping in his chest like a

294

machine-gun and he felt a pain.

'Sir?'

He sank down onto a step. Breathless, he managed with an effort to say,

'Get flashlights, quick.' He had to pause for breath before he added,

'This is it. This is where he's been taking them.'

'Can you see anything, sir?'

O'Hara shook his head slowly. It was an effort, but he got it out in the end.

'No. I don't have to. Believe me.'

He waited. The pain was like a stake driven into his chest and radiating down his left arm.

By the time Rhew got back, with uniforms in support, O'Hara had been absolutely immobile for ten minutes. He felt weak, legs trembling as he stood up, sweating. He reached out his right hand.

'Give me a flashlight.'

It was a powerful beam, used by the crews of highway patrols. It cut through the blackness like a searchlight.

The light beam swept a circular room that had been built over a hundred and fifty years before, playing over the old walls and the ascending wooden benches where students had once sat and watched operations.

Tom O'Hara's chest felt as if it was being squeezed in an iron corset.

More beams pierced the blackness like a battery of searchlights, moving in all directions.

Nobody spoke.

And then as one beam made the gruesome find, the others clustered around it, as if searchlights had bracketed an aircraft.

In the well at the centre of the room was an ancient wooden operating table, like a rectangular butcher's bench, with old leather straps hanging loosely from the sides.

But what the pools of light gathered on, that brought a horrified silence, was the outline of human shapes on the wooden surface, outlined by the recent blood that had sprayed and leaked from them.

The victims.

30

She awoke in her bedroom that morning — or was it early evening? The drapes were drawn, the bedside lights were on.

Her head ached, and the taste in her mouth was vile. She gazed up at the ceiling, blinked several times, and closed her eyes again. It felt as if she had had an anaesthetic.

Had she had an operation? The headache grew worse.

The first strange thing happened when she tried to massage her forehead. Her arm wouldn't move.

Obviously she'd been lying on it. But then the other wouldn't move either.

Into her fuzzy disturbed mind came a fear. Swallowing, she made to get up.

She couldn't. And her legs wouldn't respond.

The fear grew alarmingly. Was she paralysed? Her neck felt dreadfully bruised. Had she been in an accident — was it, God forbid — broken?

She seemed to be on some sort of table, the bed pushed aside. That was strange. Jean felt sick, and her eyes refused to focus properly.

But something dark swam into her vision,

297

loomed over her, grew larger.

Her focus improved and the dark blur took shape. It confirmed her worst fear that she had had an accident.

The head was dressed in the latest surgical scrubs, with hood, mask and smock. Only the surgeon's eyes were showing.

Eyes.

Then she saw the terrible madness.

Jean Hacker screamed as the nightmare threatened her sanity. She fought to get free, twisting and bucking, ignoring the pain of the securing ropes as they bit into her wrists and ankles.

Then it happened, stilling her as if venom had reached her brain; a low hiss of a chuckle that emanated from the surgical mask.

'It's no good, you know.'

She sank back, sobbing.

'Please — please let me go. This is not right. Let me go now, while there's no harm done. Please.'

He chuckled, came nearer again, gently placed a hand on her breast. Jean couldn't stop herself flinching. She saw the anger fire into his eyes — eyes that she thought she knew so well, but were now so alien.

He inclined his head, mockingly.

'That will change, Jean. Soon you will long for *my* caress.'

She saw the knife in his other hand, watched it come slowly, point first, towards her throat.

'What I need, my darling, is the sweetness of your pain, the most powerful of all the aphrodisiacs.'

Jean stiffened, lifted her chin up, backwards as the point of the knife touched her throat. It followed until she could get no further, stayed with her.

'Such a pretty neck.'

Through her tortured mind came the thought, frightening in its own realization, of what she knew must lie ahead, and that if she had the courage she could thrust forwards, impale herself on the knife, perhaps end it all — cleanly.

If death by choking on your own blood was clean.

And she knew with a strange, unreal calmness that in comparison it would be.

But the moment passed.

His other hand left her breast, pulled the thin shoulder strap tight. The knife sliced it effortlessly. Slowly, methodically, he did the same for the other side.

Irrationally, she noted his icy detachment, the lack of passion, like a man opening a parcel.

But her own fear set her body shaking as

the knife moved to the middle of her chest. The point came down to the centre of the black satin between her breasts.

Jean struggled, pinned only by the arms and legs, but he steadied her movements by pressing on her chest with the palm of his gloved hand. He delicately traced a line straight down with the knife, its point so sharp, his control so absolute that the material parted, slid away to both sides to reveal her white skin.

Unblemished.

Not a scratch.

Not a drop of blood.

The blade stayed near the end of its run, lingering at the very heart of her womanhood.

Her head fell back as she froze, frightened of the slightest tensing of his muscles, the slightest movement that would presage the thrust into her that would mean a dreadful, all consuming pain.

And the start of death.

She whimpered.

'Please God — please. Please don't.'

He giggled. It was weird. Like a small boy.

And like a small boy suddenly losing interest — he turned on his heel, walked to the door. He looked back at her, sniggered, then, she was left alone.

Jean looked down at her naked body, at the

remnants of the black silk at her sides, throwing her white body into stark contrast.

She was nothing now but fodder — food for a maniac and his obscene taste. A large plastic sheet covered the floor underlining the awful fate awaiting her.

Tears streamed down her face.

She had meant to achieve so much, had wanted, without actually thinking of it consciously until now, to see the children of her children, to know what it was like to pass on the genetic miracle in the great relay race of mankind.

Destiny?

It was something that was now to be sooner than she had expected, destined for a grisly end to an indifferent life.

The tears flowed unchecked.

And what of James Larsson — a life so near yet so dreadfully far from her own?

As she prayed for the strength to get through her ordeal, prayed for the forgiveness of sins, she also prayed for the tormented soul of James Larsson.

31

Tom O'Hara lay on his back, dressed only in his underpants and socks.

It was cool on the doctor's couch, and he felt comfortable, the pain in his chest much better, but the tightness was still there.

From his chest led wires attached to the suction pads the doctor's nurse had applied after rubbing grease near his nipples.

The physician was studying the ECG as the paper rolled out.

The doctor nodded to the nurse, who stopped the machine and began removing the suction attachments.

O'Hara sat up, swung around, waited as the doctor wrote up his notes, taking a towel to wipe off the grease. Finally he could wait no longer and reached for his shirt.

'I've got to go, Doctor.'

The man looked startled.

'You do realize you've had a heart attack, don't you?'

O'Hara grimaced, continued dressing, pulling on his trousers.

'I rather guessed as much.'

The doctor stood up.

'You've got to take it easy, man, rest for a few days and we need to start you off on — '

O'Hara found his shoes.

'Not now. We've got to stop these murders.'

The nurse jumped as the doctor slammed his notes down onto the desk.

'Don't you understand — you'll be the one dead if you don't take care?'

O'Hara didn't pause as he pushed his feet into his shoes.

'A few hours, that's all I ask, then I'm all yours.'

The physician shook his head in despair.

'Here, take these. Break them under your tongue when you get pain.'

He held out a box of capsules. O'Hara grabbed them as he swept up his coat.

'Thanks for your help. I promise — no physical excesses.'

The doctor looked at his retreating back and realized that there was no way his patient would keep his promise. Well, it was a free country. If the man wanted to kill himself, there was nothing he could do about it.

O'Hara went straight to the computer room.

'Any result yet?'

The woman operative shook her head.

'We've had trouble with the power supply, sir, its been disrupted by the storm several times. And there has been flooding in the back-up generators.'

O'Hara turned to Rhew.

'Anything from forensic?'

Rhew, looking worried, shook his head.

'No sir. Let me get you a cup of tea.'

O'Hara scowled.

'I'm not going to peg out on the spot.'

But he had one all the same. He sipped it, looking moodily at the computer screen.

The hands on the wall clock were slow, he noticed, showing the length of time the power had been off.

Then there was a click.

The computer came into life, spewing out reams of text.

When it finished O'Hara was stunned.

One serial killer was a rarity.

Two working together was unknown — almost.

But it had happened, there could be no doubt they had joined up, become a team.

The first murders coincided with the time when one of them was resident in the cities where they had taken place, two more in the places where the other had lived.

The remaining four when they had both been living in the same area.

And now here. And the pace of killing had increased.

OK, it wasn't proof of anything, but O'Hara knew he was looking at a pattern, and patterns were powerful indicators in his experience. You could not avoid them.

This time coincidence played no part in his thinking. And the new information also explained why there was never DNA or forensic material available, or sperm.

But he was worried.

Why the increase in tempo? Why two murders so close together? Nieminen, he was probably unplanned, but two . . . What had caused them to erupt in such maniacal fury. After each of the previous killings there had been a cooling off period of months, sometimes a year. Then it dawned on him, there was only one variable.

Jean Hacker had not been around for any of the previous incidents.

And if he truly believed in what he was thinking, then she must be acting as a catalyst, driving them on in greater fury.

Or. His heart seemed to give an extra large thump, as he fully took in his thought process.

Maybe the hospital murders were a blind.

That this time *she* was the target all along.

Maybe they had only come up with this idea after the first standard killing. Or, perhaps it had come to them later when

George Nieminen had got in the way, but after Annabel's death. If Jean Hacker were brutally murdered, they would all — media and police alike — put it down to the work of the murderer who was still at large.

Which it was. Most people wouldn't draw the obvious inference — that Jean was special.

Suddenly he remembered, she lived alone . . . O'Hara reached for the phone, then hesitated. What good would it do to call her? Then he decided he must, just to say he was coming over and that it was important.

He found her number, punched the buttons. Nothing happened, no ringing tone. He rattled the rests and tried again. He tried her cell.

Nothing.

Unease began to grow at terrifying speed.

With an explosive burst of energy he just flung the telephone aside, and ran for the door, leaving the amazed operatives to swing round in their chairs, hearing him shouting for Rhew. Frightened, his sergeant followed, expecting to see the boss go down at any moment.

On the desk was his unlit pipe.

32

Time had no meaning, no measure for Jean. It could have been two minutes, it could have been twenty before she heard the stairs creaking, and then a floorboard beyond the bedroom door indicated the presence of someone close.

But the door remained shut. What was he waiting for?

Craning to see hurt her bruised neck. She flopped back. Seconds passed. Through her hopelessness Jean felt anger and called out.

'What are you waiting for?'

Her voice was hoarse.

'Why don't you get on with it?'

The moment the door handle turned, her anger left her and was replaced by overwhelming fear. She raised her head again.

And then a miracle occurred.

Into view stepped Pam Mortimer.

Jean screamed out.

'Lock the door. For God's sake you're in danger. Lock the door.'

The woman looked blankly back at her.

Jean was almost hysterical.

'Get me free.'

At last Pam moved.

Jean struggled against her bonds.

'Quick, for God's sake, he'll be back.'

The psychiatrist walked over to her, then stopped.

Jean ceased her struggling.

'Pam?'

And then something happened that was unreal. Macabre.

Slowly, deliberately, the woman began to undress.

A coldness gripped Jean.

'What are you doing, Pam? For pity's sake . . . ' Her voice died in a whisper as realization dawned.

She was the one Steven had been seeing, the one who had such a hold over him.

Pam saw it on Jean's face, knew what she was thinking, and nodded.

'Yes, I've known Steven much longer than you. I told him not to be so foolish when he said he wanted to marry you. With our tastes it could only end in disaster.'

Gently she reached out, brushed Jean's tear-stained cheek with the back of her hand, carefully lifted a skein of hair from her eye.

When she spoke it was husky, full of tenderness, as between lovers.

'I'm sorry, Jean. Believe me. I didn't want it to be like this.'

Pam Mortimer leaned forward, went to kiss her.

Jean snatched her head to one side.

'Get away from me.'

Pam jerked back, her hand a blur as she slapped Jean's face with such force that it rocked her head the other way. Without another word she picked up her fallen clothes and tossed them onto a chair.

At that moment, in the doorway, a figure in surgical scrubs, complete with head-covering and mask, stood there, back-lit by a flash of lightning coming from the landing window.

As Pam went to him, the light flickered and died.

When it came again she was putting her arms into an ER gown that the figure was holding up for her.

The house shook as thunder broke directly overhead.

The psychiatrist stepped into white theatre boots, drew a full hood like his own over her head, tucking away any wisps of hair that still showed and finally tied on her mask.

The last thing she did was to push her hands into the surgical gloves he held.

She was ready. He reached out, turned on the big ceiling light. They came then, stood either side of her, hands raised in the classic manner of surgeons holding themselves clear

309

of contaminating objects.

He selected a mouth prop from a tray of instruments all displayed on a wooden trolley that she recognized was one from the kitchen, and held it in front of Jean, so that she could see what was coming.

She felt the panic explode in her as adrenalin rocked through her body in a shock wave.

Yet despite it all she had to know one thing. At the end of her ordeal, when the pain ceased and she was released into whatever existence, if any, awaited after death, would James Larsson be waiting for her?

Or had he deserted her in her moment of need?

She looked up at the macabre figures looming over her.

'Tell me, have you killed James?'

They paused. She could see puzzlement in his eyes, so she added, 'He was here, with me.'

The eyes of her tormentors said it all as they locked together in shock.

They'd never seen him.

So, James Larsson must have walked out on her even as she was preparing herself for him.

And now she was to be butchered by the only other man in her life.

Her husband.

And his evil succuba.

33

Pam Mortimer looked down at Jean.

'She's bluffing. There was nobody here.'

Still in his ER gear, Steven Hacker made for the door, snatching off his surgical mask.

'We'll have to check. I'll get my shotgun.'

Pam Mortimer picked up a scalpel, brought it to Jean's throat as she put a hand under her chin and stretched it back.

'If you find him — kill him. He's too dangerous to play around with.'

She looked down at Jean.

'We can make it look as though he did this one.'

Jean started to struggle.

Pam Mortimer with icy indifference tightened her grip and pushed the scalpel a half inch into Jean's neck.

'Keep quiet, bitch.'

Hot blood rushed down her skin, pooled behind her head.

Rigid with shock, Jean could hardly breathe. Her eyes were wide open with terror. It was less than a hair's breadth from her carotid artery.

Steven Hacker slipped from sight. A

minute went past, turned to three.

Pam Mortimer never moved.

Nor did the knife.

Jean strained to keep absolutely still.

Far away a rumble of thunder rolled around the heavens.

*   *   *

Detective Tom O'Hara leant forward, peering through the rain-lashed windshield.

Caught in the headlights was the cause of his discomfort, a black torrent of water where normally a neat, suburban road ran alongside a stream.

The driver glanced nervously across at him.

'Can't get through that, sir.'

'Go back, try further up the hill, on Meers Avenue.'

O'Hara slumped back, felt the sweat trickling down his back, a nagging stitch in his chest.

The rain lashed the car again, driving so hard that the windshield wipers lifted from the glass and moved through water like striking oars.

Tom O'Hara held his hand to his chest.

The pain there was like a rat gnawing to get out.

The car reached Meers Avenue, started to race up the hill weaving around fallen branches.

They all saw it at the same time. An articulated truck with a trailer that had jack-knifed and turned over. It was a scene of devastation, with highway patrol cars, fire trucks and ambulances all with their flashing blue and red lights. Firefighters, paramedics and highway patrolmen were struggling in driving rain to free the trapped driver. Nearby a large tree lay on two cars.

'That's it, sir. The only other way across the gulley is to go up to the freeway, to junction thirteen and along.'

O'Hara snorted.

'It'll take twenty-five minutes — probably more, and there's no guarantee. No, there's only one thing for it.'

He started to get out. Sergeant Rhew looked at his boss in horror.

'Sir, you can't.'

O'Hara paused, looked over his shoulder.

'Yes I can, boy. Now get your arse out of there.'

With that he launched himself into the deluge.

Rhew pulled a face, muttered to the driver. 'He's going to kill himself.'

★   ★   ★

313

Steven Hacker went straight to his bedroom and pulled up with a start. His black hood was gone and the black sweater he'd been wearing. He looked around nervously then went to the wall cabinet in his dressing room. He took out a pump action shotgun, and a box of shells. Fully loaded he stepped back to the doorway, and checked the landing.

It was *empty*.

He advanced along the wall, the gun ahead of him, searching all the time for a target, eyes darting ceaselessly from side to side.

He checked all the bedrooms, reaching for the light switches as his trigger finger tightened.

They were all empty.

He moved to the top of the stairs started cautiously down, gun unceasingly probing — ready for anything that moved.

★   ★   ★

They crawled on hands and knees, under the huge tree trunk, hair plastered over their faces, clothes clinging black and sodden to their bodies.

O'Hara stood up, covered in mud. Despite his breathlessness he was away before Rhew was on his feet.

He caught up with him as he stood on a

314

cross-road and flagged a cab to a halt, its windshield wipers clacking back and forth in the beating rain, flinging water in all directions. Chest heaving, O'Hara rapped on the window, searching in his pocket as the driver wound down the window.

O'Hara held up his shield.

'Police. I'm commandeering your car.'

The startled man had no time to argue. O'Hara flung open the back door and got in as Rhew ran around and jumped into the front passenger seat.

The taxi driver did a three point turn, and back swinging, careered off into the rain.

★   ★   ★

Steven Hacker reached the bottom of the stairs, moved slowly with his back to the wall.

Gently, with the barrel of the shotgun, he eased open the dining-room door. Light came from somewhere, he could see the backs of chairs.

As the door swung gently back he caught sight of a figure. Terrified, he pulled the trigger.

The explosion rocked the room, the large wall mirror that had caught his reflection disintegrated into a million shards of flying glass.

He racked another shell into the barrel, leapt further in. Unable to stop himself Hacker blasted the room twice, the dining table's dark polished surface suddenly ripped into white pieces that stuck up like jagged fingers.

The next shot blew the large vases on the sideboard into a dust storm.

Chest heaving, he stood in the deafening silence of the wrecked room.

He fumbled in his pocket as ejected used shells rolled around the floor at his feet.

When he'd re-loaded he crept towards the living-room. If the bastard was still around, he must be there.

The door was wide open, the interior unlit.

He edged up to the black opening. The gun in his hands began to shake. He ran his sleeve over his sweating brow.

Steven Hacker took a deep breath, stepped halfway in — and froze. There was somebody behind the door.

He sniggered, pressed the barrel against the wood and pulled the trigger.

In shreds it flew back, smashed against the wall, reared up off its hinges.

But no blood seeped through the torn wood. It was the last straw. Wildly Hacker fired into the gloom, the darkness blasted apart by an explosion of sparks. He fired again, and again, the dark sofa disembowelling white foam until it pitched over onto its back.

In the returned silence the only noise was a

metal ashtray, spinning like a top on the wooden floor.

Hacker backed out of the room. Even as he turned he saw the nightmare figure emerge from the shadows.

All in black, the eyes behind the mask, *his* mask, glittered without compassion.

A killer — just as he had looked to so many — and to Jean.

Steven Hacker brought the gun up.

'Now you get yours, soldier boy.'

He pulled the trigger.

Nothing happened.

He pumped the action, tried again.

Only clicks.

The figure moved, a slow step forward, and stopped again as Hacker, hands shaking, found a loose shell left in his pocket. He racked it up the chamber, snapped the gun back, and raised the barrel.

But there was nothing there.

The nightmare figure had gone.

Steven Hacker whirled around, the sweat streaming down his face, soaking his green scrubs. He snatched the head gear off, backed away, whimpering as he jerked the gun from side to side.

He went up the stairs, still backwards, stumbling, trying all the time to see the slightest movement in the dark at the bottom.

So he never saw the black wraith rise up beside him as he reached the landing, only aware of the glittering eyes at the instant a hand came around his face, wracking his head back and bringing him onto his toes.

Caught in a last flicker of renegade lightning what followed was breathtaking in its speed.

The knife sweep was clean, from ear to ear, simultaneously severing the left and right carotid arteries. In the same co-ordinated movement it swung down and up, the blade piercing liver, spleen and lung.

The shotgun dropped to the floor, and cart-wheeled down the stairs. The hair trigger released, the blast exploding a large chandelier.

Released from the grip of his killer Steven Hacker whirled around like a dervish, blood pumping six feet into the air through his clawing hands. Then as suddenly as a puppet with the strings cut, the body collapsed to the floor, rolled off the landing and fell down the stairs.

Glass and plaster rained down like a blizzard on the red carnage, sticking to the coagulated blood.

Unmoving the killer looked down at the twitching remains of Steven Hacker, head to one side, like a cat with a maimed bird.

Watching the death throes — emotionless.

34

Pam Mortimer had kept the knife hard into Jean's neck as a succession of shotgun blasts rocked the house.

In her agony Jean prayed. There was a long delay, and then a detonation right outside the door, on the landing.

The psychiatrist jumped, the knife twitching inside Jean's neck, a fraction away from her pulsating carotid artery. The bleeding that had slowed surged again, hot and sticky beneath her. She was lying in a pool of her own blood.

The house returned to silence.

Pam called out.

'Steven?'

Her voice was hoarse.

In the distance a long slow rumble of thunder seemed to go on for ever. Just when it seemed to be finishing, a last louder crump vibrated the instruments in the trays on the trolley.

Instruments of healing.

And of torture.

'Steven, answer me.'

Her voice was higher.

Croaking, Jean somehow managed,
'Frightened Pam?'

The woman snatched a glance down at her, twisted the knife, snarled.

'You stay quiet, bitch.'

Jean choked on blood and saliva, terrorised by the pulsating artery she could feel against the hardness of the knife.

But Pam Mortimer looked away, uncaring, back to the door.

'Steven — Steven — '

Her voice died as the black hooded figure stepped into the doorway, stopped, looking, its head moving in strange, inhuman jerks.

Pam Mortimer sucked in her breath at the sight of the blood-stained knife in its hand.

She found her voice.

'Come near me — and I kill her.'

She jerked the knife, Jean's scream ending in a gurgle, like a drowning woman.

Which she was.

The apparition didn't move.

Hysterically Pam Mortimer yelled.

'Get out of here. Get out.'

The mouth in the black mask opened, showed red as it hissed.

But no other sound came.

No words.

Without warning it drew out of sight.

Minutes passed.

Pam Mortimer stared rigidly at the door.

The lights snapped off, plunging the room into total darkness.

Terrorized, she called out, voice unnaturally high,

'If you touch me, she's dead.'

Blackness.

Silence.

Suddenly her wrist was gripped by something that felt like an iron clamp.

Screaming, she put all her weight and strength into a downward thrust that would almost have severed Jean's head from her shoulders.

But it was already too late.

The iron grip slowly, inexorably lifted her hand up, then began to twist until the pain made her fingers part.

The knife clattered to the floor. As abruptly as it came, the grip was released.

Lightning flickered.

Pam Mortimer shrank back from the figure of death right beside her, and ran.

She got through the door and across the landing, and was halfway down the stairs when the lightning came again and thunder crashed.

At the bottom, in an intense and prolonged burst of blue light she saw the outstretched arms of Steven Hacker, his white plaster-covered body accentuated by the brilliant red pool of the arterial blood in which he lay, eyes fixed, staring unseeing at the ceiling.

She lost her footing and fell on top of him, his arms flapping around her.

Screaming she fought free from the obscene embrace, got to her feet. She looked back up the stairs.

The black apparition stood there.

Whimpering, Pam Mortimer fled out through the front door down the drive.

Jean lay in the darkness, wondering what was happening, what was going to happen. Would she bleed slowly to death?

The light came on.

Shortly afterwards there was a shuffling noise.

She found the hooded shape leaning over her.

'James?'

The eyes behind the slits looked down at her, but he didn't move.

An awful doubt crept into her mind.

'James, it's me. It's Jean.'

The black head tilted to one side. His hand came out, gently brushed her cheek.

She knew then that it was him.

And yet . . .

'James, take off the hood.'

The eyes looked at her, unblinking.

The moment turned into eternity. Finally

Jean closed her own, fought back the tears. Something had happened to him.

She could not feel the breeze that rippled over the surface of his conscious state, or hear the tinkling in the mind of James Larsson.

But she knew, knew that he was not seeing her but rather some body else. Knew that the man above her was in some other reality, a place of hellish torment.

She opened her eyes again. The knife was held up in front of her.

The time had come.

She could see his hand was shaking.

Love helped her.

She smiled.

'Goodbye James.'

Their eyes met for the last time.

He waited.

When she was ready, she nodded.

35

The taxi encountered a turbulent river coming down her road, and crashed into it like a landing craft.

Tom O'Hara urged the driver on.

'Keep moving, we've got to get up there.'

The engine faltered, fired again and the car jerked its way forward. As they got further up the road they climbed free of the torrent and accelerated.

Water spilling from the trees hit the car in lumps, bursting on the roof.

'Sir.'

Rhew shouted, pointed through the windshield. Faintly, right at the top of the road a figure in a surgical gown was struggling into the woods, slipping on the sea of mud.

'It's the Mortimer woman.'

O'Hara held onto the pain in his chest, and said breathlessly,

'Leave her. She's not going anywhere. I want you . . . in the house . . . with me.'

The headlights swept into the drive, picked out the wide open front door.

'Oh God.'

O'Hara had the car door open before they

came to a grinding stop throwing up gravel. But Rhew was ahead of him racing into the house, pulling up in his tracks as O'Hara caught up with him.

Together they looked down at the body of Steven Hacker, one leg on the stairs, arms outstretched, congealed blood emerging from a gaping 'mouth' beneath his real mouth, hanging like tentacles.

O'Hara snapped.

'Search down here.'

He stepped carefully past the gruesome wreckage, calling out,

'Doctor Hacker.'

The only answer was a distant rumble of thunder. Gasping, he reached the top of the stairs, saw the half-open bedroom door, and human feet on the end of a table. He pulled up, frightened at what he might see. The pain inside him seemed as if he was about to explode.

O'Hara staggered to the door, fell against it, bursting it fully open. Horrified, he saw the naked body of Jean Hacker lying on a table.

O'Hara lurched towards her, frightened by the sight of the blood around her neck.

Even as he did so she groaned, brought a hand up to her face, the severed rope that had tied her to the table hanging from her wrist.

At that moment, as Rhew ran into the

room, pain engulfed Tom O'Hara like a fire, erupting from his chest down his arms, up his neck and head. So much pain that blackness closed around him.

Merciful, pain-free, blackness.

He collapsed, knocking over the trolley of instruments, dragging a linen cloth in his fist.

Rhew dropped to his knees beside his boss, saw the grey face, the blue lips. He knew what had happened.

He ran to the top of the stairs, yelled to the taxi driver, standing in the front door, rigid with fear at the sight of Hacker.

'Radio for the paramedics — fast. We've got a cardiac arrest and a haemorrhage — then get up here. I need help.'

With that he rushed back in, started on Tom O'Hara, forcing the latter's head back and opening his jaws for mouth-to-mouth resuscitation, then applying cardiac massage. As he put his weight on the ball of his hands, he looked quickly up at Jean Hacker. There was a hell of a lot of blood around. God knew how long they'd have to wait before help arrived.

★ ★ ★

Jean came back to life in the late afternoon of the following day, the rays of golden sunshine

326

falling on the wall opposite.

She looked blankly at the drip in her arm, then felt the pain in her throat as she tried to look in the other direction.

She remembered being brought in then, her impression reinforced as a nurse bustled into the room and she caught sight of a uniformed police officer outside the door.

It all came back; the faces peering over her in the ambulance, turning to look at somebody else on the bunk opposite. They were working on him, but she couldn't see his face because of the oxygen mask.

She'd gone mad then, trying to see if it was James, her screaming as high as the siren rising and falling like the sound of a banshee wailing at the end of the earth.

Finally oblivion came as they stuck a needle in her arm.

The nurse came to her.

'Oh, you're awake. How do you feel?'

Jean tried her voice. Only a barely audible croak came out.

'OK. I want to see the police.'

The nurse nodded.

'Leave it to me.'

She went to the door. The officer stood up from his chair, glancing back at Jean as they spoke. Then he hurried away.

The nurse came back, took a thermometer

from the wall holder. Before Jean let her put it into her mouth she held up a hand, whispered.

'Can you tell me what happened?'

The nurse, like all of the hospital staff, the state, the country, thanks to the miracle of the satellite, knew of the incident at the house on the hill.

But she looked uncomfortable and hesitated.

Jean realized what the problem was.

'I know my — husband was involved. But what happened to Major Larsson?'

The nurse looked blank.

Jean bit back her frustration.

'The psychiatric patient.'

Her face registered understanding. 'Oh. They're still looking for him.'

She pushed the thermometer into her mouth.

Shocked, Jean sank back onto the pillow, mind trying to cope with it all.

So he was alive.

Later she asked,

'Who was the man they brought in with me — in the ambulance?'

She was told it was the policeman in charge of the investigation — a heart attack.

An hour later the sun was still casting long evening shadows when Rhew was shown into her room. He shook her hand, smiled down at her.

'You look healthier than the last time we met.'

She held onto his hand with both of hers.

'I want to thank you for what you did for me.'

Rhew coloured. Wan and exhausted, bruised and bandaged, she was still a very beautiful woman.

'I only called the paramedics — my boss deserves the credit for getting us there in time.'

Her face clouded.

'How is he?'

Rhew shrugged.

'I'm going to see him when I've finished here, but strictly no shop talk.'

He held up a tape recorder.

'Do you mind if I have this switched on during the interview?'

They went through the events leading up to the attack on her, Rhew finally saying with heavy emphasis —

'So you admit freely that James Larsson was at the house, *alone*, with you that evening?'

Flushing Jean looked levelly back at him.

'Yes. I left him in the living-room while I went upstairs.'

Rhew frowned, clearly troubled.

'Are you sure he wasn't one of those who attacked you?'

'Quite sure.'

'So why do you suppose he didn't resist, shout a warning, do anything when the others came up the stairs, or for that matter when you ran screaming down them trying to get away?'

Faltering, Jean looked down at her hands, tightening a handkerchief into a knot.

'He's not cured yet. He blacks out — from reality, I mean. He must have been confused.'

She glanced defiantly back up at him.

But Rhew remained silent, consulting his notebook.

'So, you came around from the blow you say your husband gave you, and they were both there, correct?'

Jean agreed.

'That's right. My husband first, then Mortimer. It was then that I asked what they had done with James. It came as a shock to them. My husband went off to get his gun.'

Instinctively her hand went to her neck and she shuddered as she added quietly.

'That's when Pam Mortimer pushed the knife into my neck.'

Rhew leaned forward.

'So it was Major Larsson who killed your

husband in a violent fight?'

Jean started to shake her head, then winced.

'I don't know. Like I said before, I thought I was going to die. That woman had a knife buried into me that could have killed me if she had moved it as little as a quarter of an inch. I was slipping in and out of consciousness. I heard bangs. Then the lights went out. When they came on again she was gone, somebody had cut the ropes. I never saw Major Larsson.'

That *was* true.

She had only seen a mask. But she knew.

'I've no idea who it was.'

Their eyes met. And she could see he knew she knew.

Rhew stood up, switching off the tape recorder.

'I'll get this typed up for your signature, Doctor Hacker.'

She asked,

'What about Pam Mortimer?'

Rhew put his chair back against the wall.

'When we find her she will help us with our investigation into several murders, and the abduction, unlawful detention and attempted murder of yourself.'

Jean's eyes widened with horror.

'*When* you find her?'

Rhew moved towards the door.

'She's been missing since the night of the storm.'

He could see the fear gripping her almost physically.

'Don't worry — we've got a twenty-four hour guard on your door.'

When he was gone she sank down into the bed.

The memory of what that she-devil had been about to do to her, capped and gowned like a surgeon from hell, brought a coldness into her body. She pulled the blanket up higher, found she was shaking.

Sergeant Rhew pushed through the doors marked Coronary Care and found the nursing sister at her station.

'Is it all right to visit my boss?'

She nodded.

'Not too long now.'

Rhew found his way to the room. Beneath banks of monitoring screens and leads, propped up into a semi recumbent position was O'Hara, wearing a flower print hospital smock. His face was grey, his cheeks pinched and sunken.

But when he saw Rhew his eyes lit up.

'Ah there you are. How's it going?'

Rhew filled him in, ending,

'I think Doctor Hacker is frightened about

Pam Mortimer still being free. Do you think I should up her protection?'

O'Hara shook his head weakly.

'No — that's not necessary. More likely you should mount a search for her body. We saw her going into that wood. If Larsson went after her, she doesn't stand a chance.'

Rhew made a note.

'I'll get onto that straight away, sir.'

'You do that. Get the helicopter with the detection equipment — that might save you a lot of time.

After he'd gone O'Hara sat chewing at his empty pipe.

Larsson would hunt her down, no doubt about that in his mind. Maybe it was for the better. What she had done to her own kind, her own sex was unthinkable. If he killed her, she would pay the price that all murderers in his youth had paid, whatever their sex.

Maybe not at the behest of a court of law, but all the same at the hands of a state-trained executioner.

★ ★ ★

Jean was dozing, the lights down low when she heard a sound.

Instantly she was wide awake.

The small wall light cast unfamiliar upward

shadows. She checked the time. It was 1.40 in the morning. The noise came again.

Jean felt the hair on the nape of her neck stiffening. Eyes fixed on the door, she reached for the button to call a nurse.

'Jean.'

The whisper seemed to come out of the very wall itself.

'Jean. Don't be afraid.'

And then he was there, a dark spectre growing and diminishing, growing again as his feet reached the floor and he finally stood up.

In her paralysed state Jean took a second to realize he'd come through the window.

She stilled her hand on the alarm button, but kept it there. Seconds passed. There was one thing that had been on her mind — eating away at her. Finally she asked,

'Where did you go, why did you leave me? And why the hood, James? Why did you put on that awful, frightening hood my husband had used?'

He stood for a long time, head bowed. Then he whispered.

'It came naturally. I found it where he had discarded it — that sort of thing has been part of my life for many years.'

He shook his head resignedly.

'I'm not *normal*, Jean. I don't know if I

ever will be again. But I would never consciously harm you. You know that, don't you?'

For seconds nothing happened, then she took her hand from the buzzer, held them both outstretched. Slowly James Larsson came forward, and sank into her arms.

Jean held on to him as great sobs racked his body, cooing gently like a mother as she stroked back his hair.

★ ★ ★

James Larsson surrendered to the startled policeman on the door of Jean's room in the early hours of the morning, and was taken away as excited crowds of newsmen and lookers-on gathered at the hospital entrance.

Rhew confronted him two hours later, just as the police helicopter got airborne carrying the heat-seeking detection equipment that could pin point living and decaying human remains by the heat they gave out.

They faced each other across a table in a bare interview room, with the recording cassette running. Rhew spoke first, giving the date and time and those present. Then he looked steadily at the man opposite.

'Did you kill Steven Hacker, husband of the doctor you have been associating with?'

James Larsson's reply was firm.

'I don't know.'

'How do you mean, you don't know?'

'I don't think you will ever be able to understand, but I'm telling you the truth. I have no recollection of events in that house after Jean left me and went upstairs.'

Rhew made it quite plain by his facial expression that he did not believe him.

Later to the question, 'do you know the whereabouts of Doctor Pam Mortimer?' Larsson gave the answer.

'No.'

Rhew later recalled in the police canteen,

'He didn't crack — never looked anywhere near to it. Special Forces interrogation training, I bet.'

The helicopter began the search pattern, flying just above the closely packed tree tops. Near the house the crew could see the road leading to it, jammed with police cars and rows of TV vans with their satellite dishes. Groups of police and forensic officers were dotted out at the front and back of the dwelling.

For a second time, Rhew questioned Larsson. Suddenly, after an hour, he noticed the sweat standing out on his prisoner's forehead.

'Are you all right?'

He received no reply.

Uneasily Rhew got up from the table, glanced at the officer with him. They moved closer to the man sitting bolt upright in his chair, eyes fixed, staring straight ahead.

Rhew moved his hand in front of Larsson's face.

There was no reaction. The eyes were locked in some far off place. Warily he reached out and took him by the shoulder, shook gently.

Larsson's head turned, looked at Rhew's hand, then slowly up to his face.

In that instant Rhew understood, knew that he didn't recognize him, knew that Larsson was looking at someone else, someone in another world; someone on the edge of a volcano. He shivered, and took his hand away.

★ ★ ★

The warning klaxon screamed out, piercing the steady roar of the helicopter.

'Contact,' yelled the observer as a red light on his panel flashed. Instantly the helicopter changed course, came back over the 'hot spot'.

The co-ordinates were radioed to the field truck. Even as they carried on with the search the co-pilot could see teams of police with dogs moving into the forest.

Relieved, Rhew lowered the phone and said to the room,

'Good news, they've got a lead. We might have found her, or a body.'

There was a cheer and somebody slapped him on the back.

But later he looked down the corridor, at the cells where James Larsson was being detained. Instead of feeling good, he began to feel lousy.

Rhew ran a hand through his hair. Jesus, what was the matter with him? But he knew the boss would feel the same way. Larsson was not the real villain of the piece. He was just as much a wounded soldier in the service of his country, as the many amputees injured by IEDs filling veterans' hospitals all over the country.

When the teams reached the 'hot spot' the German Shepherds with them became excited, nosing and rooting in the ferns and sodden earth and running around tree trunks. Guided by the scent of articles on Mortimer's clothing none of them followed any new tracks. So this was it. Police tape roped off the area as digging commenced, a series of shallow trenches extending outwards in a precise pattern from the centre of the 'fix'. Rhew arrived, stood with the State governor patiently awaiting the inevitable.

Media helicopters thundered incessantly overhead.

But the inevitable never came. By nightfall they had found nothing. Almost relieved, Rhew went home — but dropped by the hospital first, to talk to the boss.

O'Hara's bed was empty — neatly made up, his bedside stuff gone. Confused, Rhew stopped a passing nurse.

'Excuse me, what happened to Lieutenant O'Hara?'

She paused.

'Could you see the senior nurse, she should be in her office.'

Rhew found her writing at her desk. He tapped on the open door.

'Sorry to trouble you. I've just dropped in to see my boss, but he's not in his room?'

He saw it in her face even before he heard it.

'I'm afraid Mr O'Hara died this afternoon.'

Shocked, Rhew stood there, unmoving, hearing the word died, but knew it was impossible.

Fleetingly, in an odd way, he suddenly understood what sort of world James Larsson sometimes inhabited, one where fantasy and reality co-existed.

Abruptly, he turned on his heel and walked away, unwilling to let the nurse see the tears welling up in his eyes.

339

* ⋆ ⋆

Over the following months there was no sign of Pam Mortimer. It was as if, as Rhew said, she had disappeared off the face of the earth — which in a way, was true.

For the 'hot spot' indeed carried the secret of her whereabouts.

Thirty feet above the trenches they had dug, already slowly filling in with leaves and mud, a black plastic bag, humanoid in shape, was lashed to the top surface of a large branch, secured by strips of a camouflage jacket and green hospital linen, with leafy twigs threaded through. It was there when they buried Tom O'Hara, a cold wind signalling an end of the long hot summer. Rhew felt the tears trickling down his face as they lowered the casket into the dark earth to the accompaniment of the police pipers.

He looked up and was pleased to see Jean Hacker, auburn hair blowing around the shoulders of her black silk suit. And beside her, in his olive green uniform, with a black armband, was Major James Larsson. He wished them well.

No proceedings had been taken against Larsson, as there was no corroborating evidence that he had killed anybody.

Furthermore, the death of Steven Hacker

was in any case judged by the District Attorney to be justified homicide, by person or persons unknown, committed to stop him murdering Jean Hacker, his estranged wife.

The subsequent behaviour of Larsson was also considered to be the action of a man with mental illness, diagnosed by a State Psychiatrist brought in by the D.A.

If he had anything to do with the demise of the murderess Pam Mortimer, and there was still no body, there was again no evidence to implicate him.

The only thing attested to by Jean, was that she had been with him shortly before the two had attacked her.

To the media, Larsson was a hero.

The shape was still there when Mrs O'Hara took a last look around the greenhouse. She fought back the tears when she found a tobacco pouch down the side of the seat in the corner.

She left it there, walked back up the neat concrete path to her car and the waiting removal truck.

Six months later James Larsson was invalided out of the army, took a job with the Park Services, as a Ranger and conservationist in a State a thousand miles away.

His wife of four months, Jean, found employment in a private medical practice. They lived in a converted barn on the edge of another forest.

Occasionally, in the deep far tracks of the bear-infested woods he would sometimes smell the scent of roses, and hear a tinkling noise and a ripple of light, triggered by the sparkling, sun-kissed water of the mountain streams.

The episodes occurred less and less frequently as the years passed.

Only once did Jean ask him about Pam Mortimer, and her fear of the woman's return. They were on a back-packing vacation, looking out over the Pacific Ocean at the setting sun, a flaming red orb lowering into a purple sea.

His arm around her shoulder gave a gentle squeeze.

'She will *never* harm you again.'

It was said softly, but there could be no doubt about its finality. She never brought up the subject again.

Promoted, Rhew grew a small moustache. A baby boy born to his wife was christened Tom.

That first year Christmas snow came and went and still the humanoid shape with its accompanying twigs, tattered camouflage and green linen strips lay on its branch. Such 'burials' by some South American Indians lasted a lifetime.

In the beginning curious animals had nibbled and burrowed their way into its delicious, rotting contents, and thousands of ants had formed columns that marched into its succulent depths.

Later, large birds, wings flapping as they steadied themselves, stabbed at the carcass with their beaks.

Finally, the head worked free of its shroud and the face showed through, still covered by the remnants of a surgical cap, the eyes staring out of the putrefying flesh.

But the sockets were soon empty, the glittering eyes that had looked down without pity on Annabel and all the others plucked out by hungry crows.

The neck muscles rotted and the vertebrae, already disconnected — smashed by one powerful blow — parted, and the head fell to the forest floor.

In the March gales other pieces of the skeleton blew far and wide.

Among the swirling leaves the rolling skull was picked up by a large fox and carried into its underground lair.

Pam Mortimer grinned in the darkness of her tomb.